FIRST IMPRESSIONS

Chloe came back down the aisle with a big grin on her face and Max at her heels. "I'm in!" she said. "Max said okay. My dad said okay. We're all set."

"Good!" Carole replied. It would be awful to prepare for a ride like this and then not be able to go.

"And don't worry about anything," Chloe said earnestly. "I'm only doing this as a prep for the Old Dominion Hundred-Mile Ride in a few weeks, so I really, honestly, truly don't care how I finish. I'll be able to teach you guys a lot."

Lisa blinked. Her overall impression of Chloe was not good. First Chloe had laughed at her, and now she was almost saying that she expected The Saddle Club to do poorly. How could she say that when she didn't even know them? How could she draw instant conclusions like that? Lisa was insulted.

Looking at the faces of her friends, Lisa could see that they felt the same way.

Other *Skylark Books* you will enjoy
Ask your bookseller for the books you have missed

THE WINNING STROKE (American Gold Swimmers #1)
by Sharon Dennis Wyeth

COMPETITION FEVER (American Gold Gymnasts #1)
by Gabrielle Charbonnet

THE GREAT DAD DISASTER *by Betsy Haynes*

THE GREAT MOM SWAP *by Betsy Haynes*

BREAKING THE ICE (Silver Blades #1) *by Melissa Lowell*

SAVE THE UNICORNS (Unicorn Club #1) *by Francine Pascal*

THE SADDLE CLUB

ENDURANCE RIDE

BONNIE BRYANT

A SKYLARK BOOK
NEW YORK • TORONTO • LONDON • SYDNEY • AUCKLAND

RL 5, 009–012

ENDURANCE RIDE

A Bantam Skylark Book / August 1997

ISBN 0-553-48424-9

Published simultaneously in the United States and Canada.

PRINTED IN THE UNITED STATES OF AMERICA

OPM   0 9 8 7 6 5 4 3 2

I would like to express my special thanks to Kimberly Brubaker Bradley for her help in the writing of this book.

1

"RISE AND SHINE, beautiful Belle, I've got some oats for you," Stevie Lake sang to her horse. At the magic word *oats*, the bay mare swung her head over the partition of the temporary stall she was in. Stevie and her two best friends, Carole Hanson and Lisa Atwood, laughed. Belle whickered eagerly as Stevie poured the oats into her feed tub.

"And Max says horses don't understand English," Lisa said with a shake of her head.

"It's hard to believe sometimes," Carole agreed.

"But it's true; they don't." Max, the girls' riding instructor, came down the dark aisle bundled in a hooded sweatshirt. In the Virginia hills, it sometimes grew chilly at

1

night, even in the summer. "They understand breakfast," he explained. "Belle can smell the oats, that's all." An eager grin lit his face. "Do you guys feel ready for today?"

This was the day all of them, including Max, were going on their first endurance ride. Endurance riding was an offshoot of English riding: The point was to cover fifty miles of rough trail in twelve hours, with a healthy horse at the end. Endurance rides were races. The fastest horse that finished in good condition won. The girls, however, were not at all worried about finishing first. They just wanted to finish.

"Sure," Carole replied. "We did our last hill work on Wednesday, as you know, and Starlight's heart rate and respirations—"

"Stop!" Stevie cried. She put her hands over her ears. Carole had been talking like this for weeks. "I know all this technical stuff helped get Belle in shape, but I absolutely can't listen to another word of it. Riding a horse is an art, not a science!"

Stevie was certainly more artistic than scientific. Her favorite kind of riding, dressage, was almost like a dance between rider and horse. Stevie's personality was artistic, too. She showed incredible creative flair, both at getting herself into difficult situations and at getting herself out. Life was never boring with Stevie around.

2

Carole blinked. "I suppose you're right, Stevie. All the numbers we've been paying attention to do make riding seem like a science." She turned back to Max. "Let's just say we're ready, that's all. I think we're really ready."

Of the three of them, Carole was the most dedicated rider. She planned to spend her life around horses somehow. She loved learning anything new, and training for endurance riding had been fun to her. Carole had read books on the subject, and she and Max had plotted a training regimen that they all had carefully followed. Starlight, Carole's horse, was in the best shape of his young life. So was Carole.

"Fair enough," Max said. "I feel ready, too." He turned and went down the aisle to the stall where Barq, an Arabian gelding, was waiting for his breakfast. Barq was a lesson horse from Pine Hollow Stables, which Max owned and where the three girls usually rode.

"I don't think Prancer's ready," Lisa said mournfully, shaking her can of oats outside Prancer's stall. "She doesn't even smell the oats. She's still asleep."

Lisa didn't have her own horse, but if she could have had one, it would have been Prancer, a beautiful Thoroughbred Max had bought from a racetrack. Prancer's willingness to learn had enabled her to become a good saddle horse in a fairly short period; likewise, Lisa's hard work had enabled her to learn about riding quickly. She was still a little behind her two best friends, but she was catching up fast.

"I can't blame her," Carole said, looking over Lisa's shoulder at the sleeping mare. Prancer dozed on her feet, her eyes shut. "After all, it is only four A.M."

Stevie groaned. "Don't remind me. It's way too early."

"You know that horses need to have time to digest their food before they're ridden," Carole reminded her.

"I know. And since the ride starts at six, we have to feed them now." Stevie shook her head. "What I don't understand is why the ride starts at six."

"So all the riders can be off the trail before dark," Carole said.

"But it's summer!" Stevie protested. "It doesn't get dark until late! Besides, you don't really think this is going to take us all twelve hours, do you?"

"It might," Lisa said. "I'm a little worried. Fifty miles is a long way, and we've never done anything like this before."

Carole put her arm around Lisa's shoulder. "We've trained for it and we're riding with Max," she said. "Besides, we're The Saddle Club. We can do anything."

Lisa felt better. Long ago, right after she had met Stevie and Carole and they had realized how horse-crazy and utterly compatible they all were, they had formed The Saddle

Club. Members had to be horse-crazy—of course—and had to help each other out. The Saddle Club had had a lot of adventures, and now that Carole had reminded her, Lisa felt sure they could also handle the endurance ride.

They knew that Max would be with them every step of the way. Endurance rides had strict rules about young participants. All riders under the age of sixteen had to be sponsored by an adult rider who would remain with them on the trail at all times.

Lisa rattled her can of oats invitingly. "Prancer . . . Prancer, darling . . ." The mare woke up and pushed her nose toward the can of oats. Lisa giggled. "Prancer's awake."

"That's more than I can say," came another voice that all three girls immediately recognized as belonging to Stevie's boyfriend, Phil Marsten. Phil materialized out of the shadows, rubbing sleep from his eyes. "I'm really not sure getting up this early is necessary," he said, "but Mr. Baker and Max say it is, so here I am." He dumped some oats into a bucket for Teddy, his horse, then rubbed Teddy's mane while the horse ate.

Mr. Baker arrived on Phil's heels. "Where's Max?" he asked. "I've got coffee." Mr. Baker owned a stable near Willow Creek, where Pine Hollow was, and led Phil's Pony Club, Cross County. At the end of the school year, Mr.

Baker had challenged Max to take part in this endurance ride. The Saddle Club had thought it sounded like fun and asked to come along. When Phil had heard what was happening, he'd asked to ride, too. The Saddle Club had met Mr. Baker many times at Pony Club events, and they liked him.

"This endurance ride was a good idea," Lisa told him, "but I really can't believe we're here." She looked around at the stables bustling with riders and horses. Not long ago, she hadn't even heard of endurance riding. Fifty miles in twelve hours sounded like an amazing amount of riding to her, but now she knew that some rides were even longer, up to one hundred miles in twenty-four hours.

Of course, she reminded herself, they wouldn't do the whole fifty miles without stopping. There were two veterinary checks on the way—places where the horses could rest and be thoroughly examined, and where the riders could grab a quick snack.

Max came back and happily accepted some coffee. Mr. Baker offered his Thermos to the girls and Phil. Carole shuddered. She couldn't stand the taste of coffee.

"My mother doesn't like me drinking it," Lisa said politely. Stevie just grimaced and shook her head.

"No thanks," Phil said. "I don't want to stay awake. This is too early! I'm going back to bed."

6

"Sorry," Mr. Baker said cheerfully. "We're packing the tents before we leave." Since endurance rides always began early in the morning, riders arrived the night before, checked their horses in, and camped out overnight. This ride started at a fairgrounds, so there were nice campsites and decent temporary stalls for the horses. Because Max sponsored an overnight ride every year, he had tents they were all using.

"Breakfast first," Max suggested. "I brought Max's Morning Madness." This was his famous homemade granola.

Everyone followed Max out to his horse trailer. He rummaged through a plastic cooler in the tack compartment, took out six small plastic bags of granola, and handed them around. They ate standing up. Lisa felt like she was already having to endure hardship. Where were the bowls and spoons? Where was the milk? Wasn't there anything to drink?

Stevie leaned forward and rummaged through the cooler. She pulled out a juice box and handed it to Lisa. "Here," she said. "You have a parched look on your face."

"Has anybody noticed the other riders?" Carole asked in an undertone. "Some of their equipment looks different."

Stevie shook her head. The night before, there had been a big spaghetti dinner as preparation for the ride, but The Saddle Club hadn't really talked to anyone outside their group. There were nearly a hundred participants; last night, when they were all wearing blue jeans and eating pasta, everyone had looked pretty normal to Stevie.

"Everyone seems more relaxed than at a horse show," Lisa observed.

"That's because horse shows are all about winning," Carole said. "I mean, I don't think they are, but most people do. Endurance rides seem to be more about finishing."

Lisa nodded. "I just want my belt buckle." Everyone who completed the ride got one.

Phil sat down on the damp grass and leaned his head against the trailer. "So do I," he said. He yawned. "I sort of wish we hadn't stayed up so late last night. I have to admit, though, Stevie, your last ghost story was pretty funny."

Stevie, Carole, and Lisa exchanged glances. They hadn't wanted Max to know how long they'd sat around their campfire. It probably would have been smarter to have gotten some sleep.

Max rolled his eyes. "I heard you, believe me," he said. "Tent walls aren't that thick. If you had started singing, I would have come out and protested, but the ghost stories weren't bad."

They laughed. Max was a good but stern teacher, and he ran the stables with a firm hand. However, he was always coming up with fun new activities, and he was very nice about most things.

"I'm getting used to no sleep at all, anyway," he told Mr. Baker jokingly. "New baby. Maxi gets us up two or three times a night."

"Then you'll have an advantage over me," Mr. Baker joked back. "I'm not used to being sleep deprived. But I figure you'll have the advantage over me anyway—I saw that nippy little Arab you brought."

"Ahhh," Max said, as if admitting a great advantage. "Barq. Yes, Arabs are excellent endurance horses. The last several world champions, I believe, have been of Arabian descent." He rubbed his hands together. "I think Barq will continue the noble tradition of the desert horse."

"Is that why you chose Barq?" Lisa asked. She'd been wondering why Max had picked a plain lesson horse over one of his more elegant Thoroughbreds.

"Partially," Max said, now serious. "Arabs tend to do well over rough trail, and they are easier to get fit than some breeds."

"He didn't want to work as hard as I've had to, getting poor Dominic ready for this," Mr. Baker said mournfully. Dominic was his horse, an elegant and sweet-natured paint gelding. Paints were always descended from Thoroughbreds

9

or quarter horses, and they were always a mixture of two colors. Dominic was brown and white. He was beautiful, but he was a lot heavier than Barq. Carole could see why it might be harder to get him into shape.

"You'll be eating our dust," Max assured Mr. Baker, smiling broadly.

"Oh-ho!" Mr. Baker said. "We'll have to see about that. I bet I'll finish in better shape than your horse."

"You personally?" Max asked.

"Of course me personally. I've been through rigorous training. I haven't eaten a single cheeseburger in the last week." Mr. Baker grinned.

"What a sacrifice!" Max exclaimed. "I'm sure I can't beat you if you went to such great lengths to prepare." He hung his head in mock defeat. The girls giggled.

Carole kept thinking about how a horse's conformation might make it more or less suited to endurance riding. "Barq is built sort of like a marathon runner," she said. "No, think about it, Stevie," she added, when Stevie laughed. "In horse terms, Barq is more like a distance runner. Dominic is like a basketball player—big and strong but not too muscular. Prancer looks like a ballerina, and Belle would be . . . I don't know . . ."

"Field hockey?" Stevie suggested. "Water polo?"

"Belle's more like Prancer, but not quite as delicate,"

10

Carole persisted. "Starlight—he's more of an all-around athlete. Like a decathlete. Teddy . . ." She paused, thinking of Phil's chunky but athletic quarter horse. "He's like a football player."

"How did you know?" Phil asked in mock amazement. "I've been teaching him to play quarterback. I was going to surprise you at the next joint Pony Club meeting." Everyone laughed, including Max and Mr. Baker.

"Come on, Stevie, I think Teddy will do better than Belle," Phil continued. "In fact, I think we'll beat you. Care to make a bet?"

Carole drew in her breath and rolled her eyes at Lisa. The only person on earth possibly more competitive than Stevie was Phil. Both always wanted to be first, best, and right. They had nearly broken up because of it several times.

"No," Stevie said, with surprising firmness. "I've learned a lot about endurance riding lately, and I know enough to know that I'm not racing anybody. Belle and I have worked really hard, and I think she's fit enough to do this comfortably, but I don't think she's fit enough, and I don't think she's experienced enough, to be racing anybody. Not even you. The people who do this all the time can go out and try to win. I just want to finish."

Carole was so proud she nearly clapped. For once Stevie

11

had gotten the better of her natural competitiveness. The three of them, and Max, had been riding for miles every day for the past few weeks. Their horses were in good shape, but not as good as the horses that did this all the time.

"All kidding aside, Stevie's right," Max said. "We're not trying to beat each other, Phil. Mr. Baker and I are kidding. We challenged each other to prepare for this ride, and to do it. Our challenge ends at the starting line."

Phil looked frustrated. "Everybody is making too big of a deal out of this," he said with a sidelong glance at Mr. Baker. "I ride Teddy almost every day, almost always on trails, for miles. I take him to Pony Club rallies. We jump. He's in super shape."

"I think a little more preparation might have helped you," Mr. Baker told him solemnly.

Phil blushed and looked at the ground. Carole didn't blame him; she knew how embarrassed she'd feel if Max ever had reason to say that to her. "I'd better check on Teddy," Phil mumbled. He set his juice box down and headed for the stables. The girls trailed after him.

Phil went into Teddy's stall. First he hugged his horse; then he gave the girls an angry look. "Look at him," he said. "Do you see any fat? He's pure muscle."

"He looks great," Lisa said honestly. It was true. Phil loved Teddy as much as any of them loved their horses, and he took excellent care of him. The gelding was a picture of health and contentment.

"Mr. Baker's like Max," Stevie said, trying to comfort Phil, "always wanting to teach things. I bet he just wanted you to understand how the really serious riders train their horses."

"Sure, I understand it, I just don't think I have to do it," Phil retorted. "Look, how hard can this be? We've got twelve hours to go fifty miles. That's barely more than four miles an hour. Horses walk faster than that. This is going to be *easy*."

"Don't forget," Lisa warned him. "The two vet checks are at least half an hour each."

Phil rolled his eyes. The longer he looked at Teddy, the happier he seemed to get; he appeared to be forgetting Mr. Baker's reprimand. "Okay, so we have to go four and a half miles an hour," he said. "Big deal. Besides, I'm not trying to win. I'm really only trying to beat one rider—a certain person named Stevie Lake. And I think Teddy and I can do it." He flashed his usual impish smile at Stevie.

"Look," Stevie said, with a slight edge in her voice, "I think you're being silly. I don't want to race you, but if I

13

did, I know I'd beat you. Belle could beat Teddy in her sleep. All our training might not have been necessary, but I'm sure it helped."

Lisa flashed an agonized look in Carole's direction. Stevie's competitiveness was making a comeback.

"You must not be that sure," Phil said, "or you wouldn't be backing out of a bet."

"I'm not backing out, because I was never in," Stevie said. "I don't need to bet to know Belle's the better horse. She's going to beat Teddy by miles—and when she does, she'll be in better shape than Teddy was when he got started."

"Let's go see if Max needs help with the tents," Lisa suggested brightly. She had a sinking feeling about the direction Phil and Stevie's conversation was taking. Diverting their attention seemed the only hope.

"Excuse me," a young girl said.

They all turned around. A girl about their age, with brown hair tied back in a ponytail, and wearing a baggy sweatshirt, stood near them. She seemed upset about something.

"I'm Chloe," she said. "I saw you guys last night, but I didn't get to talk to you. My horse is stabled next to the bay over there—it says 'Starlight' on the card on the stall."

"You've got the gray horse, then," Carole said. "Starlight's mine. I'm Carole Hanson."

Chloe bobbed her head politely in Carole's direction. "I've got a big favor to ask you," she said. "See, my dad was coming on this ride—he was going to be my sponsor—but a few minutes ago his horse cut its coronet, so the horse can't go, so my dad can't go, so I can't go, see?"

The Saddle Club nodded. Chloe needed an adult sponsor. The coronet was the ring of flesh just above a horse's hoof, and even small cuts there could be serious.

"So I figured you guys must have a sponsor," Chloe continued.

"Max, our riding instructor," Lisa said. "And Mr. Baker, Phil's instructor."

"Do you think I could ride with you?" Chloe asked. "Could Max sponsor me? I know what I'm doing—I've already gone over a thousand miles."

15

2

"Wow," Lisa said, impressed. "You drove a thousand miles just to get to this ride? Where did you come from, Michigan?"

Carole elbowed Lisa in the ribs just as Chloe, despite her worried expression, started to laugh. Lisa looked puzzled. "She means miles of endurance rides," Carole explained. To Chloe she added, "So, you've already finished twenty rides?"

"Not quite," Chloe replied. "They weren't all fifty-milers. I've done some hundred-mile rides, too."

There was something in the way she spoke that was not quite bragging but was close. Of course, Carole thought, if

16

I'd done a zillion endurance rides, I'd be proud of myself, too. Still, she could see that Chloe's laughter had made Lisa feel embarrassed.

"Do you want me to take you to Max?" Carole asked. "He's over by our trailer." She pointed to Max.

"The tall man in the baseball cap? I'll go myself." Chloe walked away.

"I just didn't know what she meant," Lisa said.

"Don't worry about it," Stevie comforted her. "Neither did I."

"Ah, yes, inexperienced riders," Phil drawled. "Course, I think the horse is more important than the rider today." He reached out to stroke Belle's neck. "Poor Belle. Your rider doesn't seem to have much confidence in you."

"I've got all the confidence I need," Stevie said, pushing Phil away from her horse and giving Belle a hug. "You're annoying me, Phil, but I don't care because I know my horse is definitely going to finish better than yours."

"Is that a bet?" Phil asked.

"I'm not betting," Stevie said, "but it's a promise."

Lisa sank her head into her hands. Stevie had just made a bet even if she didn't call it that. She was going to try to beat Phil. "That's the second thing we have to endure today," she whispered to Carole. "Stevie and Phil trying to outdo each other."

17

Carole looked puzzled. "What was the first thing?"

"Breakfast. No spoons. No milk."

Carole shook her head. "Breakfast was the second thing. Sleeping in that wind tunnel was the first."

Lisa laughed. The flap on their tent had been broken, and somehow they had been perfectly positioned so that every passing overnight breeze had blown inside.

Chloe came back down the aisle with a big grin on her face and Max at her heels. "I'm in!" she said. "Max said okay. My dad said okay. We're all set."

"Good!" Carole replied. It would be awful to prepare for a ride like this and then not be able to go.

"And don't worry about anything," Chloe said earnestly. "I'm only doing this as a prep for the Old Dominion Hundred-Mile Ride in a few weeks, so I really, honestly, truly don't care how I finish. I'll be able to teach you guys a lot."

Lisa blinked. Her overall impression of Chloe was not good. First Chloe had laughed at her, and now she was almost saying that she expected The Saddle Club to do poorly. How could she say that when she didn't even know them? How could she draw instant conclusions like that? Lisa was insulted.

Looking at the faces of her friends, Lisa could see that they felt the same way. Phil folded his arms across his

18

chest, Stevie looked indignant, and Carole looked stunned. Only Max looked normal. Maybe he was too old to feel insulted by a rider Chloe's age.

"Why would you say that?" Carole asked stiffly. She didn't know much about endurance riding, but she knew so much about other types of riding that she thought it sort of balanced out. Of course, Chloe wouldn't understand that. But why would she assume they didn't know much? It was rude.

Chloe looked at them and seemed surprised. "This is your first endurance ride, isn't it?" she asked.

"Yes," said Stevie, "but why would you think so?"

Chloe laughed. "Well, Max told me, but I would have guessed anyway. I thought so last night when I saw you. I mean, look at you!"

The Saddle Club looked. They saw their usual selves. They weren't dressed for the ride yet—in fact, they were wearing the jeans and sweatshirts they'd had on the night before—but Chloe wasn't dressed for the ride yet, either. Their horses' stalls weren't as spiffed up as they would be for a Pony Club rally, but all their equipment was neat and in order. The horses looked great. Just who did Chloe think she was?

Max didn't seem to notice Chloe's astounding arrogance or the way it had stunned The Saddle Club. He grinned

19

and clapped Chloe lightly on the shoulder. "I know I'm supposed to be responsible for you," he said, "but with your experience, maybe you don't need a sponsor."

Oh, please, Lisa thought, hoping that maybe the ride organizers *would* let Chloe go on her own.

"Oh, no," Chloe assured him. "I absolutely do need a sponsor. It's true that I've got enough miles to ride without one, but if I do, even once, they'll move me out of the junior division forever. I don't want to ride in the adult division yet. I'm leading the points in this region for the juniors right now, but I wouldn't be able to catch the adult points leader."

Max gave a little shake of his head. Carole thought that maybe he hadn't expected Chloe to take him seriously. "Wow," he said. "I can tell you really know endurance riding. I'm sure we'll do fine."

"I'm sure we will," Chloe said. "I promise, I don't care how fast we go. All I want to do is have my horse finish in twelve hours. I'll go just as slowly as you all need."

If you looked at it analytically, thought Lisa, who was good at looking at things analytically, there was nothing truly insulting about what Chloe was saying. She hadn't called them names or made fun of their horses. She hadn't laughed—except when Lisa hadn't understood her. She seemed genuine, forthright, and sincere.

20

Yet somehow, despite having just met them, she assumed they knew absolutely nothing, and she was treating them like babies. Even Max. That, Lisa decided, was very insulting indeed. It didn't help that Max seemed so impressed with Chloe, either.

Earlier in the morning Lisa had had doubts about her ability to complete the endurance ride, but now, in the face of Chloe's contempt, she had none. Hadn't they ridden for hours on end before, on mountain trails, in forests, on beaches? Hadn't they been training for this ride for weeks? How hard could this be? As Phil had said, they only had to go four and a half miles an hour. Lisa was profoundly sorry that Chloe was going with them on the ride. From the looks on Carole's and Stevie's faces, she could tell they felt the same way. Phil also looked disgusted. Only Max had retained his usual expression of calm.

Stevie was rigidly angry. She couldn't believe Max had let this Chloe person come along. He could have pretended it was against the rules. He could have said, "I'm sorry, I have an obligation to the riders from my own barn—who are, you know, quite fabulous riders, capable of any trail in the country, as am I." That would have put Chloe in her place. Instead, Max was actually smiling at Chloe as though it were some sort of honor to accompany her on the ride!

21

Phil pulled Stevie away before she could speak. "Geez, is she a pain!" he said. "You and I might argue over who's best, but at least we don't think we're better than the rest of the world."

"I can't believe Max is letting her come with us," Stevie moaned.

"I'm sure he didn't realize she's a pain until just now," Phil said. "But listen, it doesn't matter to you and me. Mr. Baker is my sponsor, remember, and he can be yours, too. You can ride with us. We'll go so fast that Chloe will have to eat our dust."

Stevie grinned. "Don't forget, Phil Marsten. You're going to have to eat mine."

CAROLE FLIPPED UP the side of her saddle to tighten the girth—the last step before mounting. She yawned and moved her hand to cover her mouth before tugging the girth a few holes tighter. Maybe those ghost stories really hadn't been a good idea.

They had changed for the ride, packed their tents and gear, and tacked up their horses. The endurance ride was about to begin, and they were ready to go.

Carole led Starlight out of his stall and down the aisle to the grassy area where their tents had been. Stevie and Lisa were already there, doing a last check of their tack and equipment. Carole swung her stirrups down, checked her

23

girth again, and mounted. Chloe led her gray horse out to meet them.

All four girls looked at each other and stared. Lisa gawked, Stevie giggled, and Carole clapped her hand to her mouth to smother her laughter. Then Carole realized that Chloe was also trying not to laugh. She felt a little stab of annoyance. *They* all looked normal. It was *Chloe* who looked weird.

Carole was wearing riding breeches, the way she normally did. Instead of her more formal tall black riding boots, though, she'd opted today to wear ankle-high paddock boots. She thought they would be more comfortable in the long run. Lisa was wearing old breeches and what Carole recognized as her old pair of tall riding boots— Carole knew they were loose and comfortable. Stevie, as always, was wearing jeans and cowboy boots. All of them wore light jackets over their T-shirts, and fanny packs that they'd bought just for the endurance ride, to carry candy bars, drinks, and spare hoof picks in case one of the horses got a stone in its foot on the trail. And of course they were all wearing the velvet-covered protective helmets Max insisted his riders always use. Their horses were wearing their usual saddles and bridles.

Chloe looked like a rider from a science fiction movie. Stevie was grateful that she wouldn't be riding in her company. Carole, looking Chloe over closely, began to feel the slightest bit intrigued. Lisa thought Chloe was just embarrassing.

Chloe's saddle was not shaped like a usual saddle. It was a weird, flat, pancake-shaped thing that didn't even look like it was made out of leather. A plastic saddle? Her stirrups were broad and flat—similar to the Western stirrups The Saddle Club used out West—but they had little wire cages over the front of them. Carole had never seen anything like them. She guessed that the cages would prevent Chloe's feet from going all the way through the stirrups in a fall—which could be very dangerous—but was Chloe really a bad enough rider that she worried about that? Carole knew keeping your heels down was usually all that was necessary.

Chloe's horse's bridle was made of plastic, too—only it was a neon-pink plastic that glowed against the horse's white hair. It perfectly matched Chloe's neon-pink plastic riding helmet. Chloe herself was wearing tights, a loose tunic, and a pair of sneakers. Several pieces of equipment hung from her saddle, but the only thing Carole recognized was a sponge.

"What's that thing on your back?" Stevie asked in a strangled voice. Chloe turned to show them. She was wearing a strange-looking nylon backpack that had a little plastic tube extending over her shoulder and around to her face. "What's the tube for?" Stevie continued.

"It's a water-filled backpack," Chloe explained proudly. "I just got it for my birthday. See, I can take a sip from the tube whenever I want, without having to use my hands."

"We've only got regular drinks—the kind that take at least one hand," Lisa said. She privately felt that she'd rather go thirsty the entire ride than wear one of those things. The tube looked like something astronauts used to speak to Mission Control.

Chloe smiled. "Don't feel bad about it," she said. "Only really serious endurance riders have these."

"Okay," Stevie said, "we won't."

Max and Mr. Baker brought their horses out of the barn. "Hey, Chloe, you look like an expert," Max said.

Chloe grinned, clearly pleased by his praise. "You should wait to see me on the trail before you say that," she said. "Anybody can buy stuff—the experts know how to ride."

Max smiled back. "Somehow I think my opinion won't change," he said.

Max had told Carole a zillion times, in a zillion different ways, that he thought she was a talented and conscientious rider. *So why does it bother me that he just complimented Chloe?* Carole asked herself. *If he'd said that to Lisa or Stevie, I'd be happy for them.*

26

"You'll have to give us some tips on the trail," Max continued.

"Oh, I'd be really glad to," Chloe said.

Stevie nudged Belle closer to Starlight. "Great! Now she has Max's official permission to brag. What was he thinking?" she whispered.

Carole shook her head. "I know what Chloe's going to say next," she whispered back. " 'It doesn't matter to me how slow—' "

"Remember, I honestly don't care how slow we go," Chloe said. Carole rolled her eyes.

"Good," Max said cheerfully, "because we will probably go pretty slow."

"Speak for yourself," Mr. Baker told him congenially. "I'm planning on *very* slow."

Stevie saw Phil at the edge of the tent, straightening a strap on Teddy's bridle. She watched him look up and noted the exact instant he took in Chloe's attire. His expression changed to one of amazement and glee.

"Oh, man," Phil said, losing control of himself entirely and laughing out loud as he brought Teddy closer. "Some people really take this stuff too seriously!" He gave another hoot of laughter. "Where're you planning on riding, Chloe? Over the moon? 'Hey diddle, diddle, the cat and the fiddle, Chloe jumped over the moon—' " A warning look from Mr. Baker quelled him. "Sorry," he said quickly, his laughter evaporating. "I mean—sorry. I know some people don't have leather saddles and stuff."

Lisa saw with relief that Chloe looked amused. Lisa didn't like the girl, but she wouldn't have wanted her feelings to be hurt, either. Lisa didn't know what had gotten into Phil. Usually he was awfully nice. *He must still be feeling embarrassed from the reprimand Mr. Baker gave him,* she decided, *so he's acting like he knows everything.*

"Some people don't want leather saddles," Chloe informed him. "See how comfortable your saddle feels at the end of the day."

Phil grinned. "At the end of the day, I won't be in my saddle," he said. "By lunchtime, I'll be sitting at the finish line, waiting for the rest of you to come in."

Chloe shook her head. "I'd make a bet with you on that, only I don't feel right about making such an easy bet."

A crackle of static over the PA system interrupted Phil's response. "Time to go!" Max said. He swung into the saddle and led them toward the start with a wave of his hand.

When they rounded the corner of the stables, Stevie couldn't believe her eyes. She knew there were a lot of people participating, but the starting line was packed! There were at least a hundred other horses and riders all waiting to go—and, she realized with a sinking feeling,

28

ninety-nine of them looked like Chloe: bright rainbow-colored plastic tack, tights instead of breeches, strange saddles with lumps of equipment hanging from them. Not everyone had a water-filled backpack, but Stevie counted at least a dozen.

"Look," Lisa said in a low voice, coming up between Carole and Stevie, "most of the horses look like Arabs."

It was often possible to tell which breed a horse was just by looking at it. Thoroughbreds were elegant, with long legs and long backs. Quarter horses were shorter and stockier, with short backs and thicker heads. Arabian horses had one less bone in their spines than most horses, so they tended to be the shortest-backed of all, but they had long, graceful necks and dainty faces.

Carole nodded. "They may not all be registered Arabs, but they sure look like Arabs."

"I wonder why?" Lisa said.

"Max said—" Carole began, but Chloe interrupted.

"Arabs are the perfect distance horse," she said. "They were bred for long rides through the desert. Whitey here is an Arab with champion endurance horses on both sides. That means—"

"We know what that means," Carole interrupted. It meant Chloe's horse's mother and father were both endurance horses.

29

"Max is riding an Arab," Lisa said. "That's Barq. His name means 'lightning' in Arabic."

"Too cool!" Chloe shouted. "See, Whitey's full name is White Lightning, only in Arabic. It's on his papers. Something Barq, I never can remember. Oh, that's cool. Max," she said in a louder voice. "It seems our horses are twins or something. Whitey's real name has *Barq* in it!"

Max grinned. "Too cool," he said.

"I'm dying," Lisa muttered. "Did those words really come out of Max's mouth? Stevie, where are you going?"

"Up to ride with Phil," Stevie muttered back. "Sorry to desert you guys."

"It's okay," Carole told her. "If we could desert us, we would."

"Do you think . . . ?" Lisa asked.

"No," Carole answered without hesitation. "Somebody has to ride with Max or Chloe will take him over. And if I have to, you have to."

"And if I have to, you have to," Lisa agreed. "Besides, I'm not sure riding with Stevie and Phil would be an improvement. What's with Phil today?"

"He didn't do much preparation for the endurance ride, because he didn't think he needed to," Carole said promptly. "Now he's worried that he was wrong, so he's trying extra hard to prove that he's right."

Lisa shook her head in amazement at her friend's perception. "That's exactly it, I'm sure—but how did you know?"

"Simple. I thought about how Stevie would be in the same situation."

Lisa sighed. "I know. They are alike, aren't they? I hope Stevie doesn't try anything stupid."

At a signal, the entire mass of horses and riders surged forward. "Here we go!" Carole cried. Starlight flicked his tail and eagerly mouthed the bit. The starting point was really a large, open field, and the path that led away from it was broad enough for a dozen horses to travel abreast. Far away they could see where the path narrowed, and Carole knew that it would soon start into the woods. Most of the endurance ride trail, like much of the state of Virginia, would be wooded and hilly.

Lisa rode on Carole's left side, and Chloe rode on her right. Max was beside Chloe. They kept their horses trotting well in hand, even though Starlight and especially Prancer seemed eager to move toward the front. Prancer had been a racehorse, and her instincts told her to fight to be first. She tossed her head and tried to break into a canter. Lisa steadied her. Already the huge group of riders was beginning to break up: Some, clearly advanced, pushed toward the front. Others hung back.

"Come on!" Phil urged, sending Teddy into a small gap

in the group of horses in front of him. "Stevie, Mr. Baker, come on!" Phil grinned from sheer excitement. Teddy wanted to move forward so badly that it was actually difficult to hold him back—and Phil didn't want to hold him. He lightened his grip on the reins, and Teddy trotted faster.

"Wait up!" Stevie said, laughing. Mr. Baker followed her. Phil had found an open space toward the front of the mass of horses, and Stevie and Mr. Baker fell in beside him. "Belle feels like she wants to gallop!" she told Mr. Baker.

"So does Dominic," Mr. Baker said, laughing but sitting back in the saddle to slow his gelding down. Dominic broke into a canter. The more Mr. Baker asked him to slow down, the more slowly Dominic cantered, but he seemed unwilling to trot. At last the horse gave in and trotted. Mr. Baker patted his neck, and Dominic tried to canter again. Mr. Baker, Stevie, and Phil all laughed.

"Teddy wants to gallop, too, but not that badly," Phil said. "This is fun!"

Farther back, Lisa and Carole were also laughingly restraining their excited horses. Prancer shook her head and whinnied loudly. Only Barq and Whitey seemed calm. Carole loosened her reins and Starlight dove forward. *It might be better*, she reasoned, *to let him work out some of his high jinks at the start. I can settle him in a few minutes, when this crowd has thinned.*

32

"I wouldn't hurry your horse if I were you," Chloe called to her. "This race is fifty miles long, you know—it's not going to be won or lost in the first ten minutes."

Carole pretended she didn't hear. She knew her horse, and she thought it was better for Starlight to go forward.

"Carole," Max said, "I agree with Chloe. Tell Starlight to whoa. Don't let him get flustered."

Carole pulled Starlight up, blushing. "But Max—"

"Whitey always used to get excited at the start, too," Chloe said. "Don't feel bad."

Carole didn't feel bad about Starlight at all—she understood his eager nature. She did feel bad that Max had corrected her, and she was beginning to feel very bad about Chloe's existence. Did the girl have to act like she knew *everything*? Carole thought about trying to explain herself, then gave up. What difference did it make, when Max had already decided to defer to Chloe the Expert on all particulars? Carole dropped Starlight behind Barq and Whitey and made a face at Lisa.

Lisa returned a sympathetic look. Leaning over, she whispered to Carole, "This is going to be a real endurance ride, all right. We're going to have to endure fifty miles of Chloe."

STEVIE, PHIL, AND Mr. Baker trotted steadily side by side. They'd been riding for nearly an hour. The path was still wide, but now it wound in and out of woods, up small hills, and down valleys. The footing remained good, and Belle seemed to feel as if she could trot forever. She was sweating lightly but looked in terrific shape. "I'll bet we've already gone ten miles," Stevie said. "We're flying."

Phil grinned. "See? I told you this wouldn't be too difficult." He reached down to pat Teddy's neck. Teddy looked every bit as fit and happy as Belle. Phil was probably right, Stevie thought. This wasn't going to be as hard as she'd thought. Max always liked to get them superprepared for everything, so he'd probably gone overboard with their training schedule. But Stevie didn't mind. She'd certainly rather be overprepared than underprepared.

"It's a gorgeous day," she said. "I just hope it doesn't get too much hotter." The sun shone bright in a cloudless sky, and there was barely a hint of breeze. She was already sweating a little bit, like Belle, and she'd drunk one of the two boxes of juice in her fanny pack. "Are you sure we're only halfway to the check?"

"I'm afraid so," Mr. Baker said. He smiled at her. Stevie smiled back. She had always liked him, even though he wasn't as easy to get to know as Max.

The trail was marked by occasional pieces of orange surveyor's tape, but the riders were still so closely bunched that most had just followed the group in front of them. Now, as they turned out of the woods, they could see several groups of riders all making their way down the side of a very large field. Far ahead, the riders disappeared into another line of trees.

"Fantastic," Phil said. "We've got all this open space. Let's canter!"

Stevie shook her head. "I don't think that's a good idea," she said. "All the books say that the most efficient gait for a horse is the trot. They can canter faster, but their canter takes so much more energy that on a long ride they're better off trotting almost all the way. After all," she added, looking at Phil, "we've got forty miles to go. And everyone says the trail gets a lot harder from here."

Phil looked back at her so sincerely that Stevie felt a flash of pride. He seemed impressed with all she'd learned about distance riding. *Even if all that conditioning wasn't really necessary for the horses,* Stevie thought, *I'm still glad Max made us learn so much. It'll be better for Belle if I ride her correctly today.*

"Stevie," Phil said in a soft voice, "you're starting to sound just like Chloe. So when will you be buying Belle that lovely pink plastic bridle?" He smirked, and Stevie involuntarily tightened her hands on her reins. Phil wasn't really impressed with her at all—in fact, he thought she was being silly.

"Or maybe, with Belle's coloring, you should consider royal blue," Phil continued. "I think I saw one of those at the starting line. It'd be all the rage at Pony Club meets— not to mention the next time you show at Briarwood." Phil signaled to Teddy and cantered away before Stevie could respond. When he cantered back, he was smiling. "I'm sorry, Stevie," he said. "I shouldn't laugh. I know you've been studying this stuff. But you should hear how funny you sound—I mean, like you said, we're not riding this to win, or to get points for the Junior Fabulous Rider of the

36

World, like that Chloe—we're just having fun. And this is fun. It's one big fifty-mile trail ride."

Stevie's indignation softened, but only a little. "You'll wish you knew all I know when Belle and I finish ahead of you," she said.

"Hah. That won't happen." Phil patted Teddy, then cantered away again. He stopped partway down the field to wait for them. Stevie, resolute, held to a steady trot, and Mr. Baker stayed beside her.

"I know I probably sound silly—" Stevie said to him.

"Not at all," he replied. "I think you're being very smart and thoughtful about this whole ride. As I said before, I wish Phil had done a little more to prepare for this than take a few extra-long trail rides."

"But do you think it will hurt him . . . or Teddy?" Stevie knew that Phil would never, ever, do anything he thought would harm Teddy. He loved his horse, and he took very good care of him.

"No, of course not," Mr. Baker said. "If I truly thought that, I wouldn't have let Phil come. Teddy's always in pretty good shape. But this is my first endurance ride, too, so I don't know everything, and I think that the more you know about any new situation, the better off you're going to be. Plus, learning is a big part of Pony Club. This ride isn't a Pony Club event in any way, but Max and I both

37

like to see our riders apply Pony Club principles to other riding situations. Always learn everything you can, Stevie. With horses, you'll find you can never know too much."

Stevie smiled. It sounded like something Max would say, and it made her feel reassured about both herself and Phil. When they reached Phil and Teddy, Phil was standing in his stirrups, looking down the trail.

"I've figured out what that line of trees is," he said. "A river! We've got a river crossing!"

LISA AND CAROLE exchanged more agonized looks—their three hundred thousandth agonized look, by Lisa's calculation, of the morning. They were trotting side by side through a nice wooded trail, behind Max and Chloe, and for the last forty-five minutes—the entire ride—they'd had to endure Chloe's endless, bragging chatter. So far she'd told them forty-seven different stories illustrating Whitey's amazing equine brilliance. Lisa thought Whitey looked amazingly ordinary, and she didn't believe half of what Chloe said. *Amazing endurance horse, my left foot,* she thought. And Whitey was a stupid name for a horse.

"When Chloe wants to go to an endurance ride, I bet she doesn't even need to load Whitey into the trailer," Lisa muttered to Carole. "A horse that smart probably loads himself. Just opens the back of the trailer, drops the ramp, and walks right in."

"Probably," Carole agreed in a low voice. "Then he turns around, pulls the ramp up, locks the door, and ties his head by the front."

"I bet he's better than that," Lisa returned. "I bet he drives the truck."

"I don't know," Carole said. "Do you think Whitey could handle a stick shift?"

"A horse like Whitey?" Lisa exclaimed. "Why, certainly."

"What was that?" Chloe asked, turning in the saddle.

"Uh—we were just admiring the shape of Whitey's hindquarters," Lisa answered, making it up on the spot. "Carole was asking if I thought he could go up really steep hills, with hindquarters like that, and I said, 'Why, certainly.'"

Chloe beamed. "He's sure got the build for endurance, doesn't he?" she said. "But, you know, he should. His grandmother is the sister of the grandmother of Rio."

Lisa didn't have a clue what that meant, but she wasn't about to say so. She was pleased to see that Max and Carole looked equally blank.

"Sorry, you've lost us," Max said politely. "Who's Rio?"

"Oh, that's right—you're not really distance riders, so how would you know? Rio is the pet name for R. O. Grand Sultan." Chloe beamed again.

Max raised his eyebrows as if impressed. "Oh," he said. "That is something."

"Who's R. O. Grand Whatever?" Lisa asked, annoyed that it still didn't make sense to her. "Remember, we're not really distance riders." She was pretty sure Chloe was incapable of forgetting that.

"I thought everyone had heard of him," Chloe said, a look of astonishment on her face.

"Not us," Carole said briefly. She ducked to avoid a low-hanging branch.

"He's one of the greatest endurance horses of all time. He's won world championships, everything. He's amazing." Chloe slowed Whitey so that she could ride between Carole and Lisa.

"That's nice," Carole said. "So he's your horse's what? Second cousin twice removed? I never can keep those things straight. Anyway, I've always thought that what a horse does is much more important than what his lineage is." Carole looked toward Max for encouragement, and he turned slightly and winked at her. She felt better. Maybe he hadn't been as impressed about the Rio thing as he'd sounded. It was Max who had taught her not to care so much about breeding.

"Sure," Chloe said. "But a horse's background can be important, too. I like to think of it as telling you what the odds are that your horse might succeed at something. I mean, if you bred two great jumpers to each other, you'd think their foal would have a better chance of being a great jumper than a foal whose parents were the two lousiest jumpers on earth."

"True," Carole said.

"So when I think of everything I want to accomplish with Whitey, I'm glad that he has a lot of other endurance horses in his family. What kind of background does your horse have?"

Carole patted Starlight's neck fondly. "He's part Thoroughbred and part quarter horse, and part we-don't-know-what, but he's all heart and good sense, and he jumps beautifully. I wouldn't change him for anything."

Chloe nodded. "He looks tough, but he's not too heavy. He could have a little Arab in him."

Carole sighed and nodded. Since she had gotten Starlight, different people had told her that he looked totally Thoroughbred, totally quarter horse, part Morgan, part Saddlebred, and part Tennessee walking horse. It always

41

seemed that people thought he was whatever breed they happened to like best. Of course Chloe would think he was Arabian. Carole didn't think he looked anything of the sort. Still, she supposed it was meant as a compliment.

Chloe turned to Lisa. "What about your mare?" she asked. "She doesn't look like an Arab."

"She's a full Thoroughbred," Lisa said, a touch defensively. "She was raced. She was going to be good, too, but she hurt her foot."

"That's too bad."

"Yeah, it was really awful for a while. See, we knew her before she got hurt, so we were really upset. No one could ride her for a long time, but she healed beautifully, and she's fine now." Lisa looked down at Prancer's shining neck and delicate head and remembered the awful day at the racetrack when The Saddle Club had seen Prancer stumble, and nearly fall, in the middle of a race.

"No . . . ," Chloe said. "I mean, what happened to her is too bad, too. It must have been terrible. But I mean it's too bad you decided to take a Thoroughbred on this ride. Didn't you say she was a lesson horse? You could have ridden something like Barq."

"I didn't want to ride something like Barq," Lisa said. "I love Prancer, and she's a great horse. I ride her whenever I can. Why would it matter that she's a Thoroughbred?"

42

Chloe shrugged. "Some of them don't handle the distance well," she said. "But I'm sure you're right—she'll be fine."

"Prancer's handled the training very well indeed," Max said, and Lisa shot him a grateful look. She knew Max wouldn't have let her take Prancer if he'd thought it was a bad idea—and even if he hadn't ridden an endurance ride before, he knew a lot about horses and riding, and he'd made sure they were all prepared. He knew what Prancer could do, and so did Lisa. Chloe didn't. Still, her words planted another seed of doubt in Lisa's mind. What if fifty miles was too much for Prancer? Lisa urged Prancer forward and rode alongside Max. For now she'd had enough of Chloe.

They rode out of the woods and across a long, flat field. Far away they could see other riders trotting, and when Lisa looked behind her, she could see more following. It was wonderful to think of so many people all doing the same competition at once. In a horse show, people mostly competed one at a time.

Lisa pointed. "Do you think those trees mean the river?" she asked.

"I'd say so," Max answered. "See how they curve along the field? They look like they're growing along a riverbank. Plus, the river's on the map, and we should be coming to it

43

about now." Lisa nodded. She remembered the map. She felt a little excited. She'd crossed streams a hundred times, but never a full-scale river.

"That's the river?" Chloe sounded nervous.

"Don't worry," Max said. "It won't be deep, and I'm sure they've made the crossing safe."

"I'm not worried," Chloe said, sounding cross. "It's just that Whitey doesn't like rivers this early. Any time we come to one in the first twenty miles, he kicks up a fuss."

"After that he doesn't care?" Carole asked.

"I know it sounds strange, but it's true," Chloe said. "It's the only thing he's bad about."

Lisa cheered up a bit. So darling Whitey wasn't perfect after all.

Sure enough, when they reached the gentle slope of land that led into a lazy, softly flowing river, Whitey refused to move forward. Chloe urged him on, patiently but firmly. Whitey snorted and trembled and attempted to whirl.

"Maybe you could lead him across," Carole suggested.

Max shook his head. "The water's too deep. Just take your time, Chloe. We're in no hurry."

"It could take hours," Chloe said with a short, exasperated laugh. "I was afraid he'd be like this."

Long ago Prancer had been wary of water, too, but she'd overcome her fear as she had grown to trust Lisa. Now she looked at the river with interest, and Lisa had an idea. "Let me give you a lead, Chloe," she said sweetly. "Have Whitey follow right on Prancer's tail, and Carole, you come right behind him." Often horses could be persuaded to do something in a group that they wouldn't do on their own. Like peer pressure, Lisa thought with a giggle.

Sure enough, Prancer splashed through the girth-deep water, and Whitey not quite as happily followed. "There!" Lisa said, once they'd reached the opposite bank. She turned in the saddle to give Chloe a smug smile. She guessed Thoroughbreds were of some use after all.

Just then Prancer stumbled. The riverbank was muddy and deep, and for a moment Prancer seemed to get one foot stuck in the mud. She staggered and regained her balance. Lisa, caught unaware, felt herself falling over Prancer's shoulder, but she grabbed Prancer's mane and held on. Prancer took a few steps forward, then limped.

"Oh no!" Right away Lisa knew what had happened. She motioned for the others to ride past her; then she dismounted into the squelchy mud. She pulled Prancer's foot up with her hands. She was right. The deep mud had acted like a suction cup, pulling Prancer's shoe right off her foot.

"Did you lose a shoe?" Max asked.

"Yes. Here it is." Lisa reached down and gingerly fished

it from the mud. The nails that held it on to Prancer's foot were twisted out of shape, but it wouldn't have mattered if they hadn't been. Only a farrier could put the shoe back on the horse.

Lisa leaned against Prancer's shoulder in despair. What could she do now? "Max," Lisa wailed, "Prancer's already started limping. She'll never be able to do this with a shoe missing." Some horses had tough hooves and never needed shoes. Prancer was just the opposite—she depended on them. Without a shoe to protect her foot from the rocks on the trail, Prancer would be in pain.

Max looked worried. "I don't know. We're right in between the start and the first check," he said. "So I guess it's best to go on. They'll have a farrier there who can nail the shoe back."

Chloe dismounted and handed Max her reins. "Let me see," she said to Lisa. Lisa moved over, and Chloe inspected Prancer's foot. "Look—the shoe came off cleanly," she said. "She didn't damage her hoof at all."

Lisa nodded. "I already saw that. But she's got such tender feet—"

Chloe smiled smugly and dropped Prancer's foot back to the ground. "Most Thoroughbreds have tender feet, don't they? And that can really be a problem on an endurance ride."

46

Lisa gritted her teeth. She wanted to hit Chloe.

"Lucky for you, she's got a pretty average-sized hoof," Chloe said. She walked over to Whitey. Lisa gave Carole a mystified glance. Just how did darling Chloe think she was going to fix this? Lisa very much doubted that Chloe had extra horseshoe nails, an anvil, and a fully trained farrier hanging from her saddle.

Chloe opened one of her odd-looking bags and pulled a strange black rubber object out of it.

"Aha!" Max said with a grin. "Chloe saves the day!"

"What's that?" Carole asked, leaning forward in the saddle to look.

"It's an Easy Boot," Chloe explained. While Lisa stared in amazement, Chloe pulled it over Prancer's bare foot and fastened it tightly. "It's temporary, but it should hold her until the vet check."

"Th-Thanks," Lisa stammered. She'd never even heard of Easy Boots before, but she was incredibly grateful that Chloe had brought one along. If the strange-looking thing worked, it would save Prancer's foot and let them all continue the ride. But *ugh*, Lisa hated to be grateful to Chloe!

STEVIE SAW THE flags for the first vet check just ahead of them on the trail and sighed with relief. She needed a break. "Here we go, Belle," she murmured as they trotted steadily along. "Fresh water. A quick bath for you. Hay."

"Hay!" Beside Stevie, Phil let out a sound that was half groan, half laugh. "I know I'm starving, Stevie, because when you said 'hay,' I actually thought, *That sounds good—a nice flake of hay!*"

"Grass or alfalfa?" Stevie inquired.

"Oh, I'm not picky. Whatever they've got the most of."

Stevie laughed and Mr. Baker smiled. "For the last three

48

miles," he said, "I've been wishing I wasn't such a coffee drinker."

Stevie understood. "It's gotten much too hot for coffee, hasn't it?" she said. Sweat kept sliding from under her dark helmet, through her hair, and down her neck. It was driving her crazy. She remembered that Chloe's strange-looking helmet had vents in it, and now she understood why. "Don't worry," she told Mr. Baker, "Mrs. Reg and Deborah said they'd bring some nice, cold sodas. I'm sure they'll let you have one of those." Mrs. Reg, Max's mother, helped him run the stable. Deborah was Max's wife.

The sound Mr. Baker made was definitely a groan.

Stevie was too proud to say it, but she already felt tired. English-style riders rose and fell with the motion of their horses' trot. It was called posting. Usually posting felt as natural and effortless as breathing to Stevie, but now, nineteen miles into the endurance ride, she was beginning to realize all sorts of things about posting she'd never noticed before. Her knees were stiff and her ankles were sore. Worse, she realized they had thirty-one miles to go.

"Let's walk," she suggested. "We're almost to the check. Let's start their cool-down now." The horses would be given a chance to get their breath back, and then they would be carefully examined by veterinarians and officials. Only those passed by the vet could continue the ride.

"Great idea," Phil said thankfully, sitting back in the saddle. Teddy dropped to a walk. His sides were moving in and out, which meant he was breathing harder than normal. Belle and Dominic were, too. The ride was hard—but not, Stevie reminded herself, harder than the training rides had been.

At the check there was a line of horses waiting. Stevie dropped to the ground and hugged Belle's sweaty neck. She was already so sweaty herself that it made no difference.

"Hi, Stevie!" A cluster of little girls surrounded her.

"Pony Tails!" she said. The Pony Tails, May, Jasmine, and Corey, were three younger riders from Pine Hollow. Like The Saddle Club, they'd formed a club based on their love of ponies.

"We came with Mrs. Reg and Deborah," Corey said. "We wanted to help out."

"Great," Stevie said. "Do you have water? Let's start by sponging Belle down." Stevie began to rinse cool water over Belle's shoulders and legs, and the little girls did the same. Deborah appeared with a bale of hay, which she set before Belle, and Mrs. Reg, to Stevie's unutterable relief, put a can of cold soda in her hand.

Almost all the riders had support crews meeting them at the checks. Stevie saw that Mr. Baker's wife was helping him, and Phil's friends A.J. and Bart were taking care of Teddy.

"We thought you'd be with Lisa and Carole and Max," May said. "We thought we'd be helping all of you at once." She pointed to the six buckets of water they had ready.

Stevie explained that she'd wanted to ride with Phil. She didn't say anything about Chloe. She knew she wouldn't be able to sound polite—and besides, Chloe wasn't her problem anymore. Stevie knew this wasn't entirely fair to Carole and Lisa, but she also knew that if they could have gotten away from Chloe, they would have.

"They must be a lot farther behind you," Jasmine observed. "We thought you'd be all together."

Stevie shrugged. She didn't think they'd gone particularly quickly or particularly slowly. Phil had urged them on, but Teddy's natural trot was slower than Belle's, so Stevie had never felt like she was hurrying. Of course, Stevie had no way of knowing how fast her friends were riding.

"I'm sure they're not far behind," she said. For a moment she wished they were all together. *Too bad Chloe had to ruin everything*—though even Stevie didn't blame her for asking Max for a sponsorship. It would be rotten to come all the way to a ride and not go. What Stevie blamed Chloe for was her annoying know-everything personality. That,

51

Stevie decided, was what was really keeping her away from her friends. She felt a rush of sympathy for Carole and Lisa, wherever they were. She was sure Chloe wouldn't improve over time.

Stevie's turn at the vet came quickly. The vet examined Belle, listened to her heart rate, and then made Stevie trot her down to a marker and back. She measured how quickly Belle's heart rate dropped afterward.

"She looks marvelous," the vet said with a grin. "You pass. Have fun."

Stevie grinned. She hadn't realized until a feeling of relief swept over her that she was actually worried about the check. Of course Belle would be fine! Stevie was thrilled to hear it, all the same.

The vet moved on to Mr. Baker's horse. As she got ready to ride again, Stevie couldn't believe the check had gone by so quickly. Jasmine pressed an orange into her hands, and Mrs. Reg stopped to pat Belle's shoulder. "She's a credit to your hard work, Stevie," she said.

Stevie glowed. Mrs. Reg had given her a compliment! That rarely happened.

She turned Belle in a half circle and watched Mr. Baker's horse complete the examination. Then she watched Phil bring Teddy in. He trotted Teddy down to the marker and back, just as Stevie had. The vet leaned over and put her stethoscope between Teddy's front legs. This was the easiest way to hear a horse's heartbeat.

The vet frowned. She glanced at her wristwatch, then listened through her stethoscope again. Finally she nodded and passed Teddy through.

Phil's face was white. He led Teddy up to Stevie and Mr. Baker and put his arm across his horse's withers. "All bets are off, Stevie," he said. "We'll just have to say you've won, because I'm not racing Teddy anymore. He barely passed the check. His heart rate didn't come down like it should have."

"Wow," Stevie said. "I'm sorry, Phil."

"Yeah, well, it's my fault," he said miserably. "Go ahead and say it, Stevie. Say 'I told you so.' "

Stevie shook her head. She felt too anxious about Teddy to be mean to Phil. "Do you want to continue?"

"What do you think, sir?" Phil asked Mr. Baker.

Mr. Baker looked at Teddy carefully. "What do *you* think?" he returned.

Phil took a deep breath. "Well, I guess the vet wouldn't have passed him if she didn't think he was okay. I know they'd rather pull a horse that might make it than pass one they don't think will. So I guess we can go on. But all bets are seriously off, Stevie, and from now on we're going more carefully. We're not going to push it."

53

"Sounds fine to me," Stevie said.

"Sounds very fine to me," Mr. Baker said. "I think you've got the right approach now, Phil."

"Yeah, well, too bad it took me nineteen miles. Let me get Teddy another drink of water, and I'll be ready to go. Stevie, I'm leaving my jacket with A.J. Do you want to leave yours?"

"No thanks." Stevie had taken hers off and tied the sleeves around her waist. It got in the way, especially with her fanny pack and all, but she had apples stuffed in both pockets to give to Belle later on.

"Here," Mrs. Baker said. She handed oranges to the three riders. They thanked her and said good-bye to their crew.

"See you at the next check!" A.J. yelled.

"Look!" May said, just as Stevie was riding away. "There's Lisa and Carole!"

Stevie stood in the stirrups and twisted so that she could see them. "Lisa, Carole! Hi! Good luck!"

"LOOK, THERE'S STEVIE!" Carole stood in her stirrups and waved. Lisa did the same.

"Gosh," Carole said as she sat back gently, "they're already leaving. Look at all the riders between us and them.

They must be at least half an hour in front of us." She was a little bit sorry that they were so far behind.

"You know, they're riding almost up with the people who are trying to win," Chloe observed. "I'd say they're going too fast."

Carole bit back a retort. How would Chloe know? "Stevie's a very good rider," she said.

"Oh, sure," Chloe said casually. "I'm sure you're all very good at riding in a ring."

"There are the Pony Tails," Lisa said quickly, before Carole could answer. From the expression on Carole's face, whatever she'd been about to say wouldn't have been polite. "Look, Carole, they've come to help Mrs. Reg crew. Look, Max! There's Deborah and Maxi."

Both Chloe and Carole looked in the direction Lisa pointed. "Are those little kids going to be your crew?" Chloe asked.

"Those little kids," Carole said, gritting her teeth, "are smart and hardworking. And they know tons about riding. In a ring and out of one."

Chloe smiled. "At the rate we're riding today, an inexperienced crew isn't going to be a handicap at all. So I wouldn't worry about that."

"We weren't," Max said. It was the first he'd spoken for

three miles. Carole, turning around, saw that Max looked a little grim. Was Chloe finally getting to him, too? Max winked at Carole and she suddenly felt much better.

"Who's your crew, Chloe?" she asked. She steered Starlight toward the waiting Pony Tails.

"My mom and dad. Just my mom was going to do both of us until my dad dropped out. Of course, we're all pretty good at doing what we have to do. My mom knows everything about endurance riding."

"Of course," Carole said, with her last shred of politeness. "I'm sure she taught you everything you know."

"Oh, no!" Chloe gave a startled laugh. "No, I taught her. I mean, my dad and I did. My mom doesn't ride."

As soon as they dismounted, all their support people rushed around the horses, making them as cool and comfortable as possible. Lisa gave Prancer's reins to Jasmine and set out to find the farrier. He quickly nailed Prancer's shoe back on her hoof.

Jasmine looked at the Easy Boot in Lisa's hand. "What's that?" she asked. "Why was it on Prancer's foot?"

Lisa explained what the Easy Boot was and how she had gotten it. Jasmine looked over at Chloe with an expression of awe. "Cool!" she said. "Lisa, she saved the day for you!"

"I know," Lisa said bitterly. "I know." *Saved the day*, she thought, *just so she could wreck it by being incredibly pompous and boring for the entire fifty miles.*

"It must be so cool riding with a girl like that," Jasmine continued. "You can tell just by looking at her that she's a real endurance rider."

"Believe me," Lisa told the smaller girl, "Carole and I are enduring plenty."

Carole came up on Starlight. "We passed!" she said happily. Then, seeing the expression on Lisa's face, she added comfortingly, "Thirty-one miles, Lisa. Only thirty-one miles to go."

Lisa nodded grimly. She knew exactly what Carole meant. Thirty-one miles until they never had to see—or hear—Chloe again.

"WAS IT SUPPOSED to get this hot?" Carole asked. She wiped yet another drop of sweat off her nose. "I didn't think it was going to be this warm today."

"It's not the heat, it's the humidity," Max said with a chuckle. Carole frowned. That seemed like such a stupid thing to say. Grown-ups were always saying things like that. What difference did a little humidity make? Sweltering heat was sweltering heat.

"Why don't you take off your jacket?" Chloe asked. "I'm going to take off mine." She stopped Whitey for a moment and removed her tunic.

Now Carole felt stupid. Why hadn't she taken off her jacket? She'd forgotten she was wearing it, that was all.

Lisa giggled. "I forgot about mine, too, Carole," she whispered. Carole felt a little better. The truth was, the trail had gotten much harder, and just plain riding was absorbing most of their attention. They were going up the face of a steep, rocky hill. Not only did Carole have to use her leg muscles to hold herself steady in the saddle, she had to continually watch the path. She didn't want Starlight twisting an ankle or cutting himself on the edge of a sharp rock.

Carole stopped Starlight on a small patch of grass just off the trail, unzipped her jacket, and took it off. The breeze on her bare arms made her feel better instantly, but she wasn't quite sure what to do with her jacket. If she folded it across her legs, it might get tangled in the reins. Usually when she wore a jacket on a trail ride, she just kept it on the whole time. *Usually,* she thought, *I don't have twenty-four miles to go.* She looked to see what Chloe was doing and sighed.

Of course. Chloe's jacket was some sort of special hiking jacket. With a few quick folds, Chloe stuffed it into its own little pouch, then hung the pouch among the bags hanging from her saddle.

Carole tied her jacket sleeves around her waist. She hated to do that—she sat on its hem every time she posted, and it bunched up funny over her fanny pack—but it sure beat wearing the thing. She wondered if her father would care if she somehow managed to lose her jacket on the trail. She decided he would.

"Rats!" Lisa said. Carole turned and laughed. Lisa was struggling with her jacket, too. "Don't laugh!" she barked to Carole. "My mother just bought me this, and I hadn't worn it riding before. I didn't know." Lisa's jacket was a pullover, and she couldn't get it off over her helmet. Prancer was standing perfectly still while Lisa went through amazing contortions, trying to yank the collar over her head.

"You know," Chloe said, "pullover styles probably aren't good for riding, at least not for endurance riding."

"Thank you, Dr. Einstein," Lisa replied sharply. "I hadn't quite figured that out myself."

Chloe looked a little upset by Lisa's words. It was the first time she had looked anything but cheerful. *Could it be,* Carole thought, *that she doesn't realize how obnoxious she is?*

"Lisa." Max's voice was sharp. "You're getting yourself into an unsafe situation. Dismount, take off your helmet, and then take your jacket off. Right now if Prancer shied, you'd have no chance."

60

"Sorry, Max." Lisa slid to the ground, and in a moment she had her jacket off and her helmet back on. "Okay," she said, looking at her jacket, "what do I do with this thing?"

Carole laughed. "Don't ask me," Max said. "I've had to tie mine around my waist, and it's driving me crazy." Lisa tied hers around her waist anyway. There was nothing else she could do.

They continued on. To Carole's dismay, the trail became even more rocky. "I'm surprised the ride organizers considered this footing safe," she said as she let Starlight delicately pick his way up the hillside. They were all walking now.

"It's bad," Chloe agreed, "but I think it's safe enough. Whitey's wearing pads, of course. Aren't your horses?"

"You mean saddle pads?" Lisa asked. "Of course."

Max cleared his throat gently. "Chloe means pads under their shoes," he explained. To Chloe he added, "No, none of our horses have them. They aren't necessary where we usually ride."

"Oh. Well, you'll want to be careful, then. I'm careful anyway. The rocks shouldn't last too much longer. Once we get to the top of this hill, I think the other side will be better." Chloe gave them all an encouraging smile. Carole wanted to puke. Chloe knew everything, it seemed, and here was poor Starlight walking on rocks without pads.

61

"Tell me about the pads," Lisa said to Max. "I've never even heard of them."

Max smiled encouragingly. Somehow, there was a world of difference between Max's encouraging smile and Chloe's. Max's actually made Lisa feel encouraged. "Don't worry, Prancer will be fine," he said. "Pads are just pieces of leather or plastic put under the shoe to protect the sole of a horse's foot. Some horses need them all the time, but most only need them if they're *usually* ridden in conditions like this. We'll be okay, Lisa. The rocks will be over soon."

"Okay." Lisa clucked to Prancer. The mare didn't seem upset by the rocks, or by anything—not even by Chloe, who was sure upsetting Lisa. Prancer was doing great.

"Hey, look," Carole cried a few minutes later, "the rocks are gone. The trail looks much better here." They were still climbing, but Carole was right—the footing did get much better.

"Good," Chloe said. "We can trot." She urged Whitey forward.

"Trot?" Lisa asked, under her breath. She was finding it hard enough to sit on a walking horse just now. Every muscle in her body ached. At Lisa's command, Prancer trotted forward willingly, her ears pricked with enthusiasm, but to Lisa it felt like Prancer's smooth stride was jarring her bones loose from their sockets. She couldn't believe she'd worn tall boots. Her feet were dying—cramped and hot. For a moment she slipped her feet from their stirrups and let her legs stretch, but that made posting so much more difficult that she couldn't keep it up. She looked enviously at Chloe's sneakers.

Riding in sneakers was usually a really dumb idea, Lisa knew. In fact, it was specifically against Max's safety rules. Sneakers had smooth soles. Any shoe with a smooth sole could slip through the stirrup if the rider fell off the horse, and the rider could be dragged. For safety, all riders were supposed to wear shoes that came over the ankle and had heels—in other words, boots. But Chloe's sneakers were special, just like all the rest of her gear. They came up snug over her ankle, and they actually had heels. Real heels. Riding sneakers. Lisa started calculating the time until her birthday. Maybe she could ask for sneakers like that. She sighed. Even if she got the sneakers tomorrow, she wouldn't be able to wear them on this ride. Her right foot especially was killing her.

Carole wished with all her heart that she'd worn tall boots like Lisa's. At the point where her paddock boots hit her calf, pressure from her stirrup leather was starting to hurt. Really hurt. It felt like she was getting blisters on both legs. She gritted her teeth and looked enviously at Chloe's sneakers. Maybe she could ask for a pair at Christmas.

Max let out a very soft groan. Carole looked over at him in alarm. He seemed to be wincing slightly every third or fourth stride. "Are you okay?" she asked him.

He grinned ruefully. "Remember the Pony Club lecture last spring on getting a saddle that fits? I don't think I was listening. This isn't the saddle I use at home; it's the one Barq usually wears for lessons. It's only an inch smaller than mine, so I thought, what does an inch matter?" He winced again. "It matters."

"Ouch," Carole said softly.

"Yeah," Max agreed. "Say, what do you think of Chloe's sneakers? I think we should all get some."

Chloe brought Whitey to a halt at the crest of the ridge. Carole, Max, and Lisa brought their horses up beside hers. "Oh, good," Lisa said. "It'll all be downhill from here."

"Real downhill," Carole said. "Look."

Chloe said, "The horses will have to slide."

Lisa looked. "Oh, Max, I can't do that," she said. The ground dropped away in front of Prancer's feet, smooth and incredibly steep.

"Of course you can," Max said. "It's only steep for a little bit. See that marker?" He pointed at some orange tape tied to a tree near the bottom of the slope. "The trail turns there and goes into the woods. Just ride absolutely straight downhill, girls. That way, if your horses slip, they can regain their feet, and they won't roll sideways and crush you. Give them all the rein they need, and trust them. They'll do fine."

"Like this," Chloe said. She clucked to Whitey, and they started down the steep slope. Chloe let the reins run through her fingers and sat far back in the saddle. Whitey tucked his hindquarters underneath him, like a dog sitting down, and actually let his back feet slide down the slope. At the bottom, Chloe gave him a pat.

"Lisa, your turn," Max said.

Lisa froze.

"Trust Prancer," Max said. "Trust yourself."

Lisa gulped but clucked to Prancer. Trusting herself— trusting her abilities—was something she worked on with her therapist. *I don't think Susan ever saw a horse slide*, she thought. She wanted to shut her eyes. But she did trust Prancer, and Max, and herself, a little. She leaned back, felt Prancer slide—and was safely at the bottom next to Chloe.

"Good girl!" she praised Prancer.

"You did well," Chloe told her. "Especially for your first slide."

65

"Thanks." Lisa turned away. Why did Chloe have to know everything?

Carole and then Max came down the slope. As they rode back into the woods, Lisa saw a funny blackish cloud hanging in the air down the trail in front of them. "Oh, yuck," Chloe said: She began to dig around in one of her bags. "Gnats. Here." She slapped some lotion on her arms, then passed it to the other riders.

"Gnats just fly around," Carole said. "Don't they?"

"These bite," Chloe informed them. She rode ahead stoically.

"The bug spray stinks," Lisa said a few minutes later.

"Yeah," Carole agreed, slapping her arms. "It bothers us, but I don't think the gnats mind it at all."

Prancer shook her head against the gnats. Lisa smacked her chin and killed three of them. The thought of dead gnats on her face made her feel sick. She wished fervently that they would come to another river. It might wash away the gnats, and, this time, bug spray and Easy Boots or not, she'd leave know-it-all Chloe and her wonder horse on the other side.

STEVIE LET BELLE have a longer rein. They had taken a slower pace ever since the first vet check, and Stevie was really enjoying the ride. They'd walked up the rocky part

66

and slid down the slide—which had seemed scary to Stevie but hadn't seemed to bother Belle. The gnats in the woods had been annoying, but they were finally past them, and in the woods it was cooler than it had been in the open sun. Now they were trotting slowly but steadily, and it felt as if Belle could trot forever.

Best of all, Stevie was really enjoying riding with Phil and Mr. Baker. Since the check, Phil had quit making rude comments and was back to being his usual funny, talkative self. Mr. Baker was surprisingly funny as well. Stevie had two new knock-knock and six grape jokes to add to her repertoire.

"Have you heard the one about the foal with laryngitis?" Mr. Baker asked.

"I'm not sure . . . ," Stevie said.

"I have," Phil answered. "He was just a little hoarse."

Stevie groaned appreciatively. "I'll have to save that one for Carole's father."

"Carole might even like that one," Phil said.

"Maybe. Her dad's the one with the weird sense of humor."

"You consider that weird?" Mr. Baker asked. "How about, What's purple and stuffed with sage dressing?"

"Tell us," Stevie said.

"The Thanksgiving grape."

Stevie snorted appreciatively.

They rode on through the peaceful woods. After a while, however, Stevie began to worry. It was a little too peaceful. "Mr. Baker," she said, "I'm not surprised we haven't been seeing the riders in front of us, because we're going more slowly. But why aren't we seeing any riders behind us? Why isn't anyone passing us?"

Mr. Baker looked concerned. "I was just starting to wonder about that myself. Have you see a trail marker lately?"

"A trail marker? No—but we have to be on the trail. It's as clear as daylight." They were able to ride three abreast along the path. "This must be right," Stevie said.

Phil's smile faded. "I haven't been looking for trail markers, either," he said. "I guess I just assumed we were right."

"Me too," Mr. Baker admitted. "But now I'm not so sure. We should have seen someone in the last few miles. And by now we should be getting close to the second vet check."

They rode on, looking closely now for the orange tape tied to the trees. Usually the trail was only marked every hundred yards or so; as Chloe had told them at the start, when you're marking fifty miles of trail, you can't leave a ribbon every six feet. Only where the trail turned or was hard to follow was it marked closely.

68

"We should have seen something by now," Stevie said at last. "Do you think we're lost?"

"Maybe," said Mr. Baker. "But I've also heard of markers being taken down before, by hikers who mistook them for litter. Let's go on a bit yet. This still seems awfully clear-cut not to be the real trail."

Finally Phil pointed and said, "Look! There's something!" A piece of pink tape fluttered from a branch.

"It's the wrong color," Stevie objected.

"Maybe they ran out of orange."

"And it's on the wrong side of the trail," Mr. Baker said. "All the markers are supposed to be to the right."

"Maybe we're going in the wrong direction," Stevie said. She felt confused and a little frightened. Could they have made a circle somehow? Could they really be lost?

"Don't worry," Mr. Baker soothed her. "No matter what, we can go back the way we came. We'll find our way out. But let's go a little farther. Maybe the pink tape was an actual marker."

"Oh no," Phil said. "Look ahead." They rode cautiously forward. Their wide trail ended suddenly at what looked like a sheer cliff face. Mr. Baker dismounted and leaned over the edge.

"It's a climbing face," he said. "You can see where rock

69

climbers have set pitons. We're on a hiking trail for humans."

"We're lost," Stevie said.

"No, we're not. We'll go back the way we came and be more careful this time." Mr. Baker remounted, and they headed back, trotting quickly but not saying a word. All of them scanned the left side of the trail for orange ribbons.

It seemed like they went several miles before they found one. All of a sudden, a cluster of orange ribbons marked the spot where they should have made a sharp turn to a smaller trail.

"Wow," Stevie said. "How could we have missed that?" She knew what had happened. They'd been having such a fun ride that they had forgotten to be careful.

Mr. Baker shook his head. "All of us should have been paying better attention. But we're on the right path now."

Stevie led the way down the narrower path until suddenly she heard Phil make an anxious squawk. She turned Belle quickly. Phil looked at her with a panicked expression. "Stevie!" he said. "Something's wrong with Teddy!"

"HE LOOKS OKAY," Stevie said. "What happened? What's wrong?"

"He's not okay," Phil insisted. "He's moving funny. Look at him." Mr. Baker rode his horse up to Teddy's side. Stevie held Belle still. Phil walked Teddy a few steps forward. "See? His back end isn't moving right."

"He looks a little stiff," Stevie said. "Not too bad, though."

"It just started happening," Phil said. His voice rose, sounding scared.

Mr. Baker dismounted. "His muscles are probably cramping," he said. "Like a runner getting leg cramps. He's sweated so much, he's probably lost too much salt. Let's see how dehydrated he is."

"Poor Teddy!" Stevie said as she and Phil dismounted quickly. She held on to Belle and Dominic while Mr. Baker helped Phil check his horse for signs of dehydration. They looked in his mouth and pulled up on his skin to see if it was getting stiff.

"He's really not too bad," Mr. Baker said comfortingly. "He's not showing any signs of major dehydration. We need to get him some salt and some more water, but I think he's going to be fine, Phil. This isn't too serious. The next vet check should be coming up pretty soon."

"If we hadn't gotten lost . . ." Phil bit his lip.

"We'd be there already, and Teddy wouldn't be cramping." Mr. Baker looked sorry. "I know."

"All of us are at fault," Stevie said.

"I know," Phil said, his voice unsteady. "But only my horse is in trouble. I've been a little worried ever since the last check."

"Did he feel stiff then?" Mr. Baker's voice was suddenly sharp with concern.

"No. No! I wouldn't have kept going. But when the vet took so long to pass him—oh, poor Teddy. I should have gotten you in better shape. I shouldn't have done this to you." Phil patted Teddy's neck apologetically.

"Better keep him moving," Mr. Baker advised gently. "He'll feel better, and we'll get to the check sooner. Don't worry, Phil. He'll be okay."

Phil ran his stirrups up on their leathers and loosened his girth. It took Stevie a moment to realize that Phil wasn't going to ride any farther. He was going to lead Teddy so that he wouldn't stress the horse any more.

"I guess endurance rides aren't that easy," Phil said as they all started moving at an even slower walk. "I should have known better, Mr. Baker. When you and Max get serious about something, there's usually a good reason."

"Don't take all the blame yourself," Mr. Baker said. "It's not all your fault, and besides, you couldn't have known this would happen."

If we hadn't gotten lost, Stevie reflected, *if we hadn't told so many grape jokes, we might have been paying more attention to the trail. Then we would have gotten to the check sooner, and Teddy wouldn't be suffering.* It seemed like a high price to pay for a couple of grape jokes.

Soon they heard the sound of a horse trotting behind them. They'd gone so long without hearing that noise that it was more than welcome. Stevie turned her head to look and saw a woman, dressed like Chloe, riding a black Arabian horse. "Whoa," she said in surprise when she saw Teddy's empty saddle and Phil walking. "What's wrong?"

Briefly they explained Teddy's problem.

"I can help a little bit," the woman said, swinging off her horse. "I've got a salt packet. . . ." She dug around in a bag that was fastened to her cantle. "Here it is. And I've got some drinking water left." She opened the lid of a water bottle hanging from her backpack and poured the envelope of salts into it. She shook the bottle, then squirted some of it into Teddy's mouth. Teddy backed away in surprise.

"Hold his head," the woman instructed. Aiming carefully, she squirted the rest of the water into the back corners of Teddy's mouth. The horse had no choice but to swallow. "There. That should help a little. Don't panic—I've done this ride three times, and we're less than a mile to the check. Do you want me to stay with you?"

"I think we'll be okay," Mr. Baker told her.

"Thanks so much," Phil called after her as she rode away.

"The people on this ride have been really friendly," Stevie commented.

Mr. Baker nodded. "Yes, but no good rider ever ignores a horse in distress."

LISA RODE INTO the second vet check with only one thought on her mind: soda. She had a can of it zipped into

74

her fanny pack, where it had been bouncing against her hips all day long and driving her crazy. Chloe and her quest for trotting had kept Lisa from stopping to drink. Now she was so thirsty that if she didn't drink her soda in the next thirty seconds she was going to die a shriveled-up human raisin. She felt like a living mummy.

"Lisa!" Jasmine, May, and Corey swarmed around Prancer. "We'll take her, Lisa," May offered as Lisa dismounted. Lisa saw that they had hay and water buckets waiting. Deborah was talking to Max, and Mrs. Reg was helping Carole. Chloe's parents were next to Mrs. Reg.

"Thanks," Lisa said gratefully. "I'll be just one second."

She unzipped the fanny pack and pulled out the can. The soda was warm—no, hot—from the afternoon sun, but Lisa didn't care. Right now, even boiling-hot soda sounded like nectar from heaven.

Lisa opened the can. The hot, shaken soda sprayed out like lava from a volcanic eruption. The first vicious, bubbling stream caught Lisa in the face. She shrieked and held the can away—and soaked the Pony Tails, Prancer, Mrs. Reg, and two of the other competitors. Corey and Jasmine screamed and ran. May, holding Prancer's reins, ducked to Prancer's far side. The competitors and Mrs. Reg scattered. Only Prancer seemed totally oblivious. She munched her hay with a tranquil expression.

75

The soda explosion settled into a foot-high fountain. Lisa looked at the mess splattered across the seat of her saddle. She felt the sticky solution dripping off her bangs. She thought about how thirsty she was. She heard a voice behind her.

"In general," Chloe said, "carbonated beverages are a bad idea on an endurance ride."

Lisa couldn't help herself. She whirled to face Chloe, and somehow—just somehow—the still-spraying soda caught Chloe in the face. "Sorry!" Lisa chirped, holding out the can. Chloe leaped backward, looking stunned. The soda stopped gushing. Lisa looked through her dripping bangs at Chloe's dripping face and shirt. She snorted, started to giggle, then lost control and laughed and laughed.

For a moment Chloe looked furious; then suddenly she was laughing, too. "I wish that had been a cola," she said. "I hate the smell of root beer."

"I'm sure it will wash off," Lisa said, wiping her eyes.

"Yeah, right. Are you really so thirsty that hot root beer sounded good?" Lisa nodded. "Then here." Chloe bent forward and offered Lisa the tube of her ridiculous water-filled backpack. Lisa drank gratefully. The water tasted sweet and almost cool.

"Thanks."

"Why didn't you say you were thirsty? I've had this all along."

"I don't know," Lisa said. Suddenly she felt a little more comfortable around Chloe. The other girl wasn't actually trying to show off, Lisa realized. She just *did* know a lot about endurance riding, and she was the sort of person who liked to talk. Even if she was driving them all crazy, she really was trying to be nice. "Sorry about the soda. I know root beer explodes when you shake it. I just didn't realize how much I'd been shaking it."

"That's okay," Chloe said. "I'm just glad you didn't hit my horse. Whitey might have thought it was a waterfall." She grinned. Lisa smiled back and went to take care of Prancer. She felt happier somehow.

Lisa soaked Prancer's legs and used a damp towel to clean the soda off her saddle. She watched Carole take Starlight through the vet check. Carole paused at the end to speak with the officials, and when she came back her face was dark with concern.

"Starlight's fine," she said in response to Lisa's unspoken question. "I just happened to see the checklist of riders, and Stevie, Phil, and Mr. Baker haven't come through the check yet."

"They must have," Lisa said. "Otherwise we would have seen them on the trail. They were really far ahead of us, remember?"

"I know. I asked the organizers, and they said Stevie definitely hadn't been through. They must be lost."

Lisa handed Prancer's reins back to May. "Let's tell Max," she said.

Max took Carole's news very seriously. He immediately went to some of the ride officials. Lisa could see them gathering equipment, getting ready to go back down the trail in search of the missing trio.

"How could we have missed them?" she whispered to Carole.

"I don't know," Carole said. "I hope Stevie's okay."

Just then Lisa saw a familiar bay mare coming out of the woods. "Carole, it's Belle! They're okay!"

TEDDY WAS ALREADY starting to improve, thanks to the salts he'd been given on the trail. Phil hovered over him, mixing more salts into a five-gallon bucket of drinking water. Mr. Baker and Stevie took their horses through the check, but Phil didn't even try. "I'm out," he said to Stevie. "Absolutely out. You win. I'm done. I wasn't ready." For once, Phil didn't seem upset about losing. He was much more concerned about his horse.

Mr. Baker looked concerned. "I really should pull out, too, and stay with Phil," he said.

"No problem," Stevie said cheerfully. "I'll just go back with Max and The Saddle Club." Max, Carole, Lisa, and Chloe had all stayed in the check much longer than they needed to, because they wanted to make sure Teddy was okay.

"We'll wait a little longer so that Belle gets a good rest," Max said.

"We aren't in any hurry," Chloe added, looking at her watch. "It's one-thirty now, and we've only got thirteen miles to go."

"That's right," Stevie said, looking up at Chloe, "you're not in any hurry, so long as we finish. Right?"

"Right," Chloe said with a grin. Stevie rolled her eyes. Lisa sighed.

"We'll be just about last," Max said. "But we'll finish in good shape, and that's all that counts."

As they got ready to go, Phil came over to say good-bye. He promised to wait at the end and see Stevie finish. "I'm sorry I was such a jerk this morning," he added.

"That's okay," Stevie said magnanimously. "You weren't really a jerk, you just didn't know what you were talking about. Teddy's okay, and that's the important thing."

"I'm really proud of you," Carole told her as they set off

79

on the final leg of the ride. "That's the first time I've seen you beat Phil at anything and not gloat about it for days. You were really gracious, Stevie."

"Oh well," Stevie said modestly. "Why rub it in? It's enough to know that this time I was absolutely, positively, one hundred percent right."

Carole and Lisa laughed. They exchanged looks they both understood. Stevie would never, ever change.

AS THEY RODE along, Lisa realized that while she might have found peaceful ground with Chloe, Carole and especially Stevie had not. Stevie was giving in to her tendency to brag, and Chloe didn't seem impressed.

"Yeah, as I told Phil, you've really got to get your horse in shape for an endurance ride," Stevie said. "I'm really glad we learned so much, Carole. It's helped a lot. Look how fresh Belle looks."

Lisa had begun to suspect that The Saddle Club still didn't know that much about endurance riding, even though she felt that she personally knew a whole lot more now than she had that morning. But she didn't say anything. She was too tired to speak.

"I think it's good you guys worked hard to condition your horses before the ride," Chloe said politely. Since Stevie had started talking, Chloe had become quieter, and her remarks had taken on a slight edge.

"Yes," Stevie said happily. "I'm sure you must spend some time working with your horse, too."

"Of course I do," Chloe replied. "But there is a little more to it than that. Your boyfriend's horse looked like a quarter horse—"

"Purebred," Stevie confirmed.

"Well, that's usually a stocky sort of horse. I was telling Lisa and Carole how conformation can have a real effect on a horse's endurance capabilities. Quarter horses are sturdy, but sometimes they heat up more quickly than other breeds. Lisa said your mare was a Saddlebred–Arab cross. I'd expect her to be better at endurance riding. It's more what she's built for. I don't think it's entirely training."

Stevie took a long, deep breath. She felt sorry for Carole and Lisa, that they'd had to endure the whole ride with Chloe. "Belle's a pretty special horse," she began, but then she didn't know what to say. She couldn't say that Belle wasn't built for endurance riding: In the first place, she probably was, and in the second place, Stevie never liked to admit that Belle wasn't fabulous at everything. But she certainly didn't appreciate Chloe's input. At least her friends let her talk without argument.

"That's a nature-versus-nurture question, and I don't think the answer matters," Max said gently. "As long as Teddy was stopped when he needed to be, and taken care of, and all our horses are still comfortable, that's what important."

"You're right, Max," Stevie admitted. She was glad that Belle seemed comfortable, because that made one of them. Stevie was incredibly uncomfortable.

"You keep wincing, Stevie. Why?" Lisa looked sympathetic.

"The inside seam of my blue jeans is rubbing holes in the sides of my knees," Stevie said. "It hurts."

"My ankles are killing me and Carole's got blisters on her calves," Lisa countered. "And Max has discovered that Barq's saddle doesn't fit his seat. You're looking kind of sunburned, too."

"It's sunny," Stevie replied.

"Chloe's got sunscreen," Lisa said. "She gave me some."

"Here," Chloe offered, taking it out and handing it to Stevie.

"No thanks," Stevie said. "I'm glad to have the chance to work on my tan."

"Are you guys really hurting that much?" Chloe asked in amazement. Carole nodded. She was riding with her feet pointed out much more than normal to take the pressure off her blisters. All that seemed to be doing was giving her blisters in new places. "Wow," Chloe said. "That's too bad. I guess having the proper gear really is important."

Up until that moment Carole had not considered any of Chloe's gear proper. Strange-looking, certainly; acceptable, maybe. But proper? Still, Chloe didn't have blisters, or sweat pouring down her face because of an unventilated helmet, and she could take a drink of water whenever she wanted one, without taking her hands from her reins. And she was wearing sneakers.

"We're battered but not broken," Max said cheerfully. "We've got—what? About another seven miles?"

"Yes," said Chloe, "and the last five are easy. The next two, though—"

"Oh, yuck," Carole groaned. She stood at the foot of a steep, rocky ridge. It looked like the trail went sideways across a small mountain. On the right side, a thin line of trees grew along the trail, and the mountain rose above them. On the left, a clifflike slope descended into a far-off valley. The riding trail in between was about ten feet wide.

"Double yuck," Chloe said. She slid off Whitey's back,

crossed her stirrups over her saddle, and gathered her reins in her right hand.

"What are you doing?" Lisa asked.

"Walking," Chloe said. "I think it'll be easier on him. It can't be much more than half a mile."

"Good thinking," Max said, dismounting and giving Barq a pat. With various groans, The Saddle Club did the same.

Lisa never minded thinking of Prancer's comfort first. That was expected of any rider. But as she climbed the slope, she reflected that tall riding boots were not made for walking. She hadn't thought her feet could hurt worse, but they did. She was also not all that keen on walking so close to a cliff edge. Riders always walked their horses on the horse's left side, and Lisa knew Prancer wouldn't like being led on the right, because it wouldn't be what she was used to. But Lisa was wary of heights, and seeing the ground fall away so quickly beside her made her feel dizzy. She tried to find something else to look at, and something besides her feet to think about.

Chloe tromped along unfazed. Carole, coming next, struggled to walk as fast as Chloe. At least, walking, her blisters didn't bother her. Stevie was thinking that her sunburn actually was starting to hurt, and Lisa was staring at

85

the back of Stevie's T-shirt and repeating the multiplication tables under her breath to take her mind off her feet and the cliff. So none of them saw what actually happened.

There was a sudden noise that made their horses jump, and then there was a thump and a yell from Max that echoed down the valley.

The girls whirled just in time to see Barq, shying sideways from something on the trail, take another sideways leap. Max was fighting to control him, but Barq's shoulder slammed into Max's chest. Both Barq and Max lost their footing and fell over the edge.

"Max!" Lisa screamed. She clutched Prancer's reins helplessly and heard her friends' screams echo in her ears. Barq slid down the slope on his side, crushing saplings and brush, his legs thrashing wildly. Max was airborne for a moment. He seemed to move in slow motion, elegantly, like a dancer. His head hit a rock. His body followed with a thump that raised dust from the ground, and he lay perfectly still.

86

9

CAROLE HAD NEVER seen a true disaster happen right in front of her eyes. Max wasn't moving. Barq scrambled to get to his feet, fell again, crashed against a boulder, and slid farther down the valley. He quit sliding and staggered to his feet, nearly twenty yards downhill from Max, then hung his head and stood still. He was bleeding.

Carole couldn't believe it. She was sure Max was going to get up in a moment, shake his head and laugh, and make some joke about looking foolish in front of his three top students. But he didn't look foolish; he looked dead. For a moment Carole's feet were frozen in place and her brain refused to think past the fact that Max wasn't moving, wasn't moving at all. She felt tears on her cheeks.

Then suddenly her feet could move again. She thrust Starlight's reins at Chloe and ran to the trail's edge. Out of the corner of her eye, she could see Stevie and Lisa doing the same thing. "Hang on, Max, we're coming," she yelled. She stepped over the edge and nearly somersaulted. She lost her balance and grabbed frantically at weeds. Small stones skittered down the slope.

"Careful, careful!" Lisa shouted, grabbing Carole's arm. They had to go slowly, no matter how desperately they wanted to hurry. Max seemed far away. Carole took another step and nearly fell again.

"Like this," Stevie said, sitting down and letting herself slide on her seat. "Like the horses did." Sliding, slipping, they reached Max's side.

He was lying on his back with his face turned to one side, his head pointing downhill and still leaning against the rock it hit. The velvet cover of his helmet was torn, and the side of it was crushed. His skin was pale, and blood from a gash on his arm poured in a steady stream onto the ground.

"Let's get his head up." Stevie grabbed his shoulder and started to pull.

"No!" Carole yelled so urgently that Stevie instantly

froze. "No," she repeated. "I had first aid in gym class last spring, remember? We can't move him. He might have hurt his back or his neck, and we could make it worse. We can't let him move at all."

"Sorry." Stevie backed away. They stared at Max, afraid to touch him.

"We have to do something," Lisa whispered.

"Right," Carole said. "Of course." She couldn't think. What came first? What had she learned? Gym class seemed like years ago.

"Carole? What should we do?" Stevie asked, her voice uncharacteristically uncertain.

"I'm thinking," Carole said. She struggled to remember. "Let's see. Breathing. He has to be breathing. That's first." She put her hand against Max's cheek. How could she tell if he was breathing? His chest would move, that's how. She looked carefully. Max was breathing.

"Okay, then; he has to have a heartbeat. That's second." She remembered how to feel for a pulse on the side of the neck and was relieved at the strength of Max's heartbeat.

"So he's not dead," Lisa said quietly. It was what they had all feared.

"No," Carole said. "He must have a concussion, like Stevie did last year. He could be hurt in other places, but we won't know until he wakes up or gets to a hospital."

89

She looked around the hillside. How would they get Max off the trail?

"I'll go for help," Lisa said. "The end of the ride isn't too far, so I'll go there as quickly as I can. They'll know what to do. You guys stay here and take care of Max—and Barq. No, really," she added when Stevie started to protest. "Prancer is the fastest horse; she and Starlight got to rest more than Belle did at the last check; and, Carole, you obviously know more first aid than Stevie or me. And Chloe's got all that trail gear—she might be able to help you. I'll go."

"Maybe someone else will come along soon," Carole said. "One of the other endurance riders."

"So many people passed us since the last check," Lisa said. "We might be the last riders on the trail. Besides, we can't wait."

"I know. Of course not," Carole said. "I just wish I knew more what to do. Hurry, Lisa! Please hurry." Lisa started up the slope.

"Be careful!" Stevie shouted after her.

At the top, Chloe listened anxiously to Lisa's account of Max's condition. "I'll ride for help if you want," she offered. "You can stay here. He's your instructor."

Lisa blinked back tears. She wanted to stay with Max,

and with Stevie and Carole. She was a little afraid of being on the trail alone, when her errand was so crucial. "No, I'd better go," she said to Chloe. "You know more about riding on trails than we do, and you're more prepared. Stevie and Carole probably need your help."

Chloe nodded agreement. "Once you get into the woods, the trail is flat from then on," she said. "You'll be able to go fast, but don't panic." Lisa nodded. To her surprise, Chloe gave her a brief hug. "Good luck."

Lisa mounted and gathered up the reins. "Take care of Max," she told Chloe. She urged Prancer forward, resisting the impulse to turn and look back. Forward was what counted. Max needed help as fast as possible.

Up to the crest of the ridge, Lisa kept Prancer to a controlled trot. She made herself hold the mare to a walk down the last steep section, even though she was dying to have Prancer gallop. No matter what, she couldn't afford to have an accident herself. Max was depending on her and Prancer.

Prancer. Lisa looked down at the gallant mare she loved so much. The horse had already traveled forty-five miles that day. Was it really fair to ask her to gallop the last five? It might be too much; it might hurt her. But Lisa knew she had no choice. Max could be dying.

Lisa urged Prancer into as fast a trot as she could. As soon as the trail flattened and she could see the woods ahead of her, she asked Prancer to run. The mare seemed to sense Lisa's urgency. She tossed her head, kicked her heels up once, and flew like the wind, doing what she'd been born and bred to do.

"HE'S BLEEDING A LOT," Stevie said, pointing to the puddle of blood forming under Max's outstretched arm. Lisa had just left, and Stevie and Carole were still bending over Max. "Really a lot," she added. "He ripped his arm on a stick. It's scary."

Carole looked and shuddered. "I didn't realize his cut was that bad," she said. "I think we need to stop it pretty quickly." Stevie pulled a wad of tissues out of her fanny pack, and in seconds they were soaked through. "Hold them there anyway," Carole instructed. "Press on the cut, but remember—"

"—don't move him," Stevie recited. "What can we use for a bandage?"

Carole looked around. "I wish our windbreakers weren't made of nylon."

"Belle's polo wraps!" Stevie said. She shouted up the slope. "Chloe! Take off one of Belle's polo wraps and toss it down here!"

Chloe already had her horse tied to a tree. She was holding Belle and Starlight, but it wasn't difficult for her to reach down and unwrap one of the long fleecy bandages that were protecting Belle's legs. She wadded the bandage into a ball and tossed it to Stevie.

Carole carefully wrapped the bandage around Max's arm. Blood soaked through the first layer, and the second, but soon the flow was at least slowed.

"I've totally wrecked one of your new wraps," Carole told Stevie.

"As if I care," Stevie shot back.

"It's bad, Stevie," Carole said in a shaky voice. "He really lost a lot of blood in a hurry."

"He'll be okay," Stevie said. "He has to be. Anyway, he's not bleeding now, right?"

"I don't think so," Carole said. Her hands were smeared red. "Stevie . . . maybe you should look at Barq? He— He's bleeding, too." They looked downhill at the patient gelding. "I'll stay here with Max. One of us has to, in case he wakes up."

Stevie didn't want to go, but she knew she should. Barq needed them, too, and she didn't think they could do anything else for Max now. "I'll help Chloe tie our horses up, and then I'll get her to help me see what we can do about Barq. Yell if you need us. Yell if anything changes."

"I will," Carole promised.

Up on the trail, Chloe was fussing with the straps on Starlight's bridle. "I'm not used to tack like this anymore," she told Stevie. "I want to tie them up, but not with the bit in their mouth. My bit snaps out."

Stevie looked at Whitey. She could see what Chloe meant. It was dangerous to tie a horse up in a regular bridle—if the horse tried to pull away, the metal bit would injure its mouth. Whitey's bridle could be converted to a halter instantly. "I'm sure we can figure out something," she said, taking Belle from Chloe. "Undo the side buckles to get rid of the bit, and make sure the nosebands are tight."

"Here!" Chloe said. "That works, and we can fasten the reins to the noseband and tie them up like that."

"Good!" Both girls worked quickly. Once the horses were secure, they removed their saddles and laid them on the ground out of harm's way. Then they looked down the hill. Carole was sitting patiently with Max. Barq looked a long way away.

"Did the polo wrap help Max?" Chloe asked.

Stevie nodded. "His arm is cut, and it was really bleeding."

"Let's take the other three down to Barq, then. Looks like he's bleeding, too."

They skittered slowly down the slope to Barq's side. He was standing on the only flat piece of ground on the entire hillside, and, fortunately, there was room for Stevie and Chloe to stand next to him. Stevie braced herself for the worst, but luckily Barq didn't seem too bad. He nosed Stevie gently.

"He's putting his weight on all four feet," Chloe said, inspecting him carefully. "He's got a lot of bumps and bruises, but he hasn't broken a leg or torn a tendon or anything like that."

"This cut is pretty bad," Stevie said, peering at the gash on his shoulder. It wasn't bleeding as heavily as Max's cut, but it was a lot longer.

"Let me see." Chloe used water from her backpack to flush some of the dirt out of the cut. It immediately started to bleed faster.

Stevie wound the polo wrap around Barq's neck and across his shoulder. It seemed to help. She added the second and third wraps down the side of his shoulder. "The rest of his cuts aren't so bad," she said. "He's lost a lot of hair, but mostly he just scraped himself. I think he's going to be okay. Look at his saddle, though." She pointed. Barq's saddle was twisted unnaturally. One stirrup had come off and the leather was ripped open in several places.

"It's history," Chloe declared. "The insides must be ruined."

"Lucky Max didn't use his good saddle. He would have hated to lose that one. And his reins snapped at the buckle. The rest of his bridle looks okay." Instead of forming a loop around Barq's shoulders, his broken reins trailed in the dirt. Stevie bit her lip and looked anxiously across the hill. Carole hadn't moved. Neither had Max.

"Okay," Chloe said, patting Barq's neck gently. "What we need to do is get this guy up with his friends. Any idea how?"

Stevie thought. "The slope is awfully steep. I know he can climb it, but he'll probably sort of lunge. I don't think it would be safe for one of us to lead him. He could knock us over without trying to."

"We've had enough of that already," Chloe said. "I agree. If we just try to chase him uphill, do you think he'll go?"

"I doubt it. How about we both lead him, one on each side, but far away? If we both hold on to a rein, we might be able to get him to climb up the hill in between us."

"That's a good idea!"

They tried, but the reins weren't long enough. When the girls held them, they couldn't get more than a few feet away from Barq—not far enough for safety.

"We need longer reins," Stevie said. "What we really need is the longe line I have for Belle at home. But maybe if we unbuckle Belle's and Starlight's reins, and only tie them with one each—"

Chloe caught on quickly. "I've got a lead rope on my saddle, too. I can tie Whitey with that, and we can use both of his reins." They gave Barq another pat for reassurance, waved to Carole, then climbed back up the slope. In a minute they were sliding down again. They tied all the reins together to make two long makeshift leads.

Now they had enough line that they could stay well away from Barq, yet still guide him. Stevie gently moved the horse so that he was facing uphill. Then they started climbing the hill, one on each side of him. When their lines went taut, they pulled gently on Barq's head, called to him, and encouraged him. Barq had always been well-mannered. He took a step forward, then another. As the slope steepened, he had to use his head for balance, and he plunged forward in halting, leaping steps. Sweat broke out across his shoulders, and he paused before each plunge as though in pain. Stevie and Chloe scrambled to climb quickly so that they could keep their reins taut and keep Barq moving.

Finally they reached the lip of the trail. Chloe sat down, gasping for breath, but Stevie stood and pulled steadily on her end of the line. "Come on, Barq, you can do it!" she said. Barq made one last leap and came up beside her. He was trembling from the effort. Stevie quickly led him away from the edge.

"Wow," Chloe said, standing up again. "We did it." They patted and praised Barq for his effort, then removed his tack as they had for the other horses. Chloe encouraged him to drink from her backpack. Barq licked the tube with seeming gratitude.

"Once he's done with that, I'd like a drink," Stevie said. "I'm—oh no! Carole wants us! There must be something wrong!" Carole was waving frantically. Without another word, Chloe and Stevie started back down the hill.

ONCE CAROLE SAW that they were coming, she went back to watching Max breathe. His chest moved in and out regularly, but that was the only reassuring thing about the way he looked.

"He looks *awful*," was the first thing Stevie said. "He looks worse. His skin's turning blue gray."

"I know," Carole said. "Why do you think I wanted you? I can't stand this, Stevie. I don't know what to do." She slid the few feet to Max's side and gently felt for his pulse again. Max was more to Carole than just the best instructor she'd ever had. He was more of a friend, or a favorite uncle.

This time Carole had more trouble finding his pulse. "There's something wrong," she said, a hint of despair in her voice. "His heartbeat's faster, but it's not as strong. I don't know what it is. I don't know what to do."

Stevie moved to Carole's side. "Don't panic. I know it's a shock to have Max hurt, but we'll get help. Now—"

"Oh," Carole said. "Oh, of course, that's it."

"What's it?"

"He's going into shock. They told us about it in first aid. We've got to put his feet higher than his head, stop any bleeding, and keep him warm."

"It's a good thing he landed with his feet higher than his head," Stevie said, "because you said we couldn't move him." She untied her jacket from her waist and put it over Max.

"Oh, good thinking!" Carole said. She did the same.

"Is he still bleeding?" Chloe asked.

"No . . . well, the cut's oozing a little, but nothing like it was." Carole looked distracted. "I don't remember what else they told us about shock. Get medical help, but we're doing that."

"Press down on his wound to make sure he's not bleeding," Chloe said. "I'll go get my jacket for him, and I'll see what else I can find."

Carole covered the bloody polo wrap with one hand. Stevie squeezed her other hand. "It'll be okay," Stevie said. "Lisa will get help soon."

"I hope so," Carole said.

"She'll do great," Stevie said. "We're doing the best we can. Max will be fine—he won't let us down. He never has."

Carole looked at Max's still form. "I don't think he has much say in it this time."

Chloe returned with her tunic, the sponge from her saddle, and all four of the horses' saddle pads. They covered Max from head to toe, and Carole fastened the sponge over Max's cut with the end of the polo wrap and continued to press down on it. Suddenly they heard Starlight whinny. On the trail above, another rider came into view—but from the wrong direction. He was a competitor, not a rescuer. As soon as he saw the horses tied on the trail, he stopped. In a moment the man had tethered his horse and was making his way cautiously to the girls' side.

"What happened?" he asked as soon as he reached them. They briefly explained. He looked very concerned. "Gosh," he said, "I don't know what else to do, either. You've already done all I can think of. Here, take my jacket. I think I'm the last rider on the trail—the friends I was riding with quit at the last check. You've already sent someone for help?"

Chloe checked her watch. "About a half hour ago."

"Maybe you could go, too?" Carole suggested. "Just in case—"

"Of course." The man slid his backpack to the ground. "Help yourselves to anything in there. There's a bandanna you could use for a bandage, and I've got some candy bars left. Sit tight. I'll be back soon." He went back to his horse and rode away.

The girls tried to find comfortable places to sit on the slope around Max. His pulse hadn't gotten any fainter. Fresh blood no longer seeped through Stevie's polo-wrap bandage. Max seemed, for now, to be holding on, but his skin was still pale and clammy, and he hadn't moved. Carole couldn't fight the uneasiness that clutched her heart. What would she do without Max?

Stevie looked inside the man's backpack. She used the bandanna to add another layer to Max's bandage. "Anybody want a candy bar?" she asked. Chloe shook her head.

"I couldn't eat," Carole said.

Stevie put the candy bars back. "Me either. It was nice of that guy to leave them for us, though. I hope he comes back soon."

"Lisa will be back long before he will," Carole said sharply.

"I know. I just meant, I hope someone comes soon." Stevie put her head in her hands. "It's been a long time since Lisa left."

Chloe checked her watch again. "Not even forty minutes," she said. "I bet it'll take her nearly an hour to finish the ride—and then it'll be an hour before anyone can make it back here. Maybe longer. I don't know if they'll be able to use horses. They might have to come in on foot."

Stevie looked at the sky. "Maybe they'll send a helicopter."

"Maybe," Chloe said.

"I got lost on the trail," Stevie said.

"Lisa won't," Chloe said firmly.

103

"I know," Stevie said. "Of all of us, she pays the closest attention to things. She'll be fine."

"I hope so," Carole said. She reached for Max's pulse again and shook her head. "He's getting weaker, not stronger. I hope some help gets here soon."

11

LISA THOUGHT THE trail would never end. Her leg muscles strained to hold her out of the saddle so that Prancer could gallop freely. She gasped for air against the wind. White flecks of sweaty foam streaked Prancer's neck and shoulders. Surely they'd galloped a thousand miles by now. She knotted one hand in Prancer's mane for balance.

"Good girl, Prancer, keep on," she murmured. She could feel the mare tiring, but even now, as she pressed her heels against Prancer's sides, Prancer responded with another surge of speed. Lisa steadied her around a corner, then burst into tears of relief. Far ahead, red plastic flags marked the finish line. People were waiting there, Mrs. Reg and

105

Deborah and a rescue squad. "Go!" she said to Prancer. Prancer plowed forward doggedly.

"Heads up!" Lisa shouted through her tears as they galloped into the clearing and across the finish line. Dismounted riders scattered; everyone looked up in surprise. Not many riders ended a fifty-mile race going as fast as their horses could run.

Lisa saw Mrs. Reg in the crowd and rode straight for her. When she pulled on the reins, Prancer stopped without argument, and Lisa tumbled out of the saddle into Mrs. Reg's arms. "Max!" she gasped. She saw Deborah, holding Maxine, standing beside Mrs. Reg, and she took a deep breath and made herself speak clearly. "Max had an accident. He's hurt badly. We need an ambulance to go get him."

Deborah's face went white. She handed Maxine to Mrs. Reg and grabbed Lisa's arm. Some of the ride officials had heard Lisa and were already alerting the waiting rescue team. Paramedics jumped out of an ambulance parked on the side of the field.

"Come on, Lisa," Deborah urged, pulling her toward them. "You'll have to tell them what happened. And you'll have to show us where he is."

Lisa nodded. "Carole and Stevie stayed with him." As

Deborah led her away, Lisa looked back over her shoulder. "Prancer . . ."

The three Pony Tails had surrounded the mare, and Lisa saw Mr. Baker and Phil coming forward as well. "We'll take care of her, Lisa," May shouted. Lisa knew they would.

She turned back toward Deborah and ran a few steps to keep up with her. "We came as fast as we could," she said. "Prancer and I."

Deborah reached back and put her arm around Lisa's shoulder. "I know you did," she said.

Two paramedics were pulling equipment out of the back of the ambulance. "Tell us what happened," one of them, a young woman with dark hair, said gently. Lisa described the accident as best she could. The woman nodded encouragingly.

"Lisa and I will go back with you," Deborah said firmly. "I'm his wife, Deborah."

The paramedics looked at one another. "Of course," the woman said. "I'm Susan and this is Daniel. We'll all go together."

The ride organizers produced a pair of four-wheel-drive vehicles. A ride steward offered to drive one for Deborah and Lisa, but Deborah assured the man that she knew how to drive it. Susan and Daniel loaded the backs of the vehicles with a stretcher and some boxes of supplies. Lisa climbed in behind Deborah, and, as Deborah gunned the engine, Lisa stood on the narrow seat so that she could get a glimpse of Prancer. The mare was wearing a mesh cooler. Mrs. Reg cradled Maxine with one arm while she held Prancer's lead rope with the other hand. May was drying Prancer's neck with a towel, Phil was sponging her hindquarters, Corey was offering her sips of water, and Jasmine was rubbing down her legs. Mr. Baker was bending over a bucket of something. Lisa sighed in relief. Surely if the mare had been in distress, the ride vets would have been crowding around her, too. Maybe the gallop hadn't hurt Prancer after all.

Deborah hit the accelerator and the vehicle shot forward. Lisa grabbed the side of her seat. "Hang on!" Deborah shouted. "The trail looks a little bumpy!" The first jolt nearly rocketed Lisa out of her seat, but she was thrilled to be going so fast. Every bump meant they were getting closer to Max.

ON THE RIDGE, the shadows were lengthening in the late-afternoon sun. The three girls kept their vigil. Max still hadn't moved. He still breathed.

"I'll go check on the horses," Chloe offered. She slipped away.

"I just wish something would happen," Carole burst out. Her arm was starting to cramp from holding on to Max's wound, but she didn't want to let go. "Waiting like this is driving me crazy." She dug a hole in the dirt with her heel.

"He's not getting worse," Stevie said. "That's something, anyway."

"It's not much," Carole replied. "And he could be getting worse, we just can't tell. I *hate* this."

Stevie didn't know what to say. Carole was rarely this upset about anything—but she certainly had reason to be upset now. How could Stevie comfort her friend when she didn't feel comforted herself? Max looked awful.

"My mom died in a hospice," Carole said. "We got to sit with her at the end, my dad and I, and it was just like this—waiting and waiting, and nothing ever changing. She didn't wake up. She didn't talk to us, or smile, or know we were there. She just *died*."

"He's not going to die," Stevie said, scooting over so that her shoulder touched Carole's. "He's just got a concussion, like I did. Remember? It was scary at first, but it was no big deal."

"I'm so scared," Carole said, her voice trembling.

"I know." Stevie thought about Carole's mother, who had died of cancer several years before. Stevie had known Mrs. Hanson a little, but she and Carole hadn't been such

109

good friends then. Mrs. Hanson had been so sick she rarely came around to the stable, and Carole never had friends over. Carole almost never talked about her mom. Stevie had never before heard what had happened the day she had died.

"What did you do at the hospice?" Stevie asked. "Did you talk to her?"

"No," Carole said, her eyes filling with tears. "I wanted to—I didn't know what to say. I didn't think it would matter. But later I thought that maybe, if I had talked to her, she would have talked back. I don't think so. The doctors gave her a lot of medicine so that she wouldn't be in any pain, and it made her sleepy. But maybe she would have said something. I wish I had tried."

"So let's talk to Max," Stevie said. "He won't die, anyway, but he might be getting bored. We may as well entertain him."

Carole let out a short laugh. "Only you, Stevie, would be trying to entertain someone who was unconscious and bleeding!"

"I tell jokes in my sleep," Stevie said. Carole shook her head.

Chloe came back. "They're okay," she said. "I gave them some water, but Belle wouldn't drink from my backpack.

She seems okay, though. Barq is getting pretty stiff, but he can still walk. I think he's just really badly bruised."

"We're going to talk to Max," Carole said in a determined voice.

"Okay," Chloe said. "Hi, Max."

"Hi, Max," Stevie echoed.

"Hi, Max," Carole said. "We're sorry you're hurt. We hope you'll be better really soon. We sent Lisa and Prancer for help, and you know how fast Prancer can run. We're expecting them any minute now."

"We figured you were probably getting bored, lying there on the ground and all," Stevie cut in. "I've got a couple of new grape jokes Phil told me this morning. What's purple and eight hundred pages long? *Moby Grape*."

"I'm really grateful to have you as a teacher, Max," Carole said. "You're the best teacher I've ever had. I've probably never said that before, but it's true."

"Thanks for letting me come on this ride with you," Chloe added. "I know a lot of people wouldn't want to take responsibility for a rider they never met. I thought you were a nice person right away, even when I saw you last night at dinner, before I needed a sponsor for the ride."

"Speaking of last night's dinner," Stevie said, "am I the only person who thinks it feels like three years ago? Carole

111

knows I'm happy to talk to you, Max, but I don't want to be too serious. If I were serious, you wouldn't believe it was me talking."

Carole smiled. "Stevie's going to say what she wants to say, and I'm going to say what I want to say."

"We're hoping she has some better jokes than *Moby Grape*," Chloe added.

"Okay," Stevie said. "Here's one. Okay, so these three strings go into TD's—"

"What's TD's?" Chloe asked.

"It's an ice cream shop near where we live," Stevie said. "If we ever get off this mountain, I'll buy you a sundae there. So the three strings go into TD's, and the waitress says, 'I'm sorry, we don't serve strings.' And so the first string goes back to his friends and says, 'Twist me up a little bit and unravel my ends.' So they do, and he goes back up to the counter, and the waitress looks at him and says, 'Aren't you a string?' 'No,' he says—"

"Starlight sees something!" Carole said. She stood up.

"No, of course the string doesn't say—oh! He does?" Stevie stood up, too, and shaded her hand against the sunlight. Starlight, Belle, Whitey, and even Barq stood at attention on the trail, their ears pricked forward in the direction Lisa had gone. "They must hear something!" Stevie said. "Let's go!"

112

"I'll take over with Max. You go ahead," Chloe urged them. Carole and Stevie hurried up the slope. They reached the trail's edge just in time to see two four-wheelers crest the top of the ridge. From the backseat of one of them, Lisa stood up and waved. Carole felt her knees go weak from pure relief.

After that, things seemed to happen very quickly. Carole went down the slope with Deborah and the paramedics to explain Max's condition. Stevie and Lisa tried to calm the horses, which were startled by the four-wheelers and a little tired of standing tied to trees. When Chloe saw that they were having trouble, she came up to help them, struggling under an armload of saddle pads and jackets.

"Not long, not long now," she soothed a trembling Starlight. She asked Stevie, "What do you think? Should we put the saddles back on? They've got blankets around Max, and I think they're getting ready to move him."

"Yeah, let's saddle up," Stevie said, nodding. "The horses will think we're going somewhere, and with any luck we will be soon. Home."

"Five more miles to ride," Chloe reminded her.

Stevie groaned. "Right. How bad is it?" she asked Lisa.

Lisa shrugged. "Not too bad, I think. I couldn't really tell, it went by so fast. I'm so proud of Prancer." She looked down the hill. "It looks like they're getting ready to put

Max on a stretcher. They've got his neck in a brace."
Whitey nudged her, and she turned her attention back to
the horses. "Oh!" she said, when she saw Barq's scraped
and polo-bandaged side. "Poor baby!" She shook her head.
"I've been so worried about Max that I didn't think much
about Barq. Will he be able to walk out of here?"

"If we go slowly," Chloe said.

CAROLE BRACED HERSELF against the slope. Deborah held
her hand tightly while the two paramedics worked over
Max. Already he had an IV line dripping fluid into his arm.
After immobilizing his neck and back, Susan and Daniel
carefully transferred him to the stretcher. Max groaned.
Carole grinned. "That's the first sound he's made," she
said.

Deborah didn't look too encouraged by it, but immediately after, as they were all getting into position to carry
Max up the hill, his eyelids fluttered once. If Carole hadn't
been looking at him she wouldn't have known it had happened, because immediately afterward he looked just as
unconscious as before, but still she felt so happy that she
nearly cried again. "He's coming out of it," she whispered.
Deborah slipped her hand into Max's and squeezed gently.
"I think he squeezed back!" she said. Even Susan and Daniel smiled.

114

When they reached the trail, they set Max down while the paramedics discussed whether or not to hand-carry him over the steep ridge. Lisa ran over. "He looks worse than he did at first," she said.

"Shock," Daniel said briefly. "His blood pressure was awfully low. If he'd kept bleeding—" He didn't finish the sentence, but Lisa didn't think she wanted him to. She shuddered. Carole looked pale.

"We're going to carry him over the crest of the ridge," Susan said. "It would be too bumpy for him on the back of a four-wheeler. After that, we'll motor him out." She looked at Deborah. "We'll handle your husband. Will you drive the four-wheeler to where the trail flattens out?"

"Sure," Deborah said.

Susan looked at the four girls. "I guess one of us will walk back for the other four-wheeler," she said.

Stevie stepped forward. "I'll drive it." To the other girls she added, "I'll be right back for Belle."

"Can you?" Susan asked.

"Of course," Stevie said, "or I wouldn't have volunteered." Lisa and Carole looked at one another. Stevie, to their knowledge, had never driven a four-wheeler in her life. "Mr. Brightstar was teaching me to drive his pickup truck the last time we were at the ranch," Stevie added. "How much different can it be?"

Deborah grinned slightly. "She'll do fine," she said.

The paramedics shrugged. "See you in a few minutes," Daniel said. They picked Max's stretcher up and started climbing.

Deborah checked to be sure the medical boxes were secure in the back of her four-wheeler. Lisa and Carole put Barq's broken saddle in the back of the other, while Stevie climbed into the seat and muttered, "Where are the reins?"

"Here." Deborah came over to Stevie's side and pointed. "Steering wheel, gas pedal, brake."

"Thanks," Stevie said.

"Keys," Deborah added. "They turn the engine on." She pushed back her hair. "I don't think those medics even realized that they were leaving four girls alone with four horses, but I do. How bad is Barq?"

"He can walk," Carole said.

"I'll lead him," Lisa offered. "I haven't got a horse to ride."

Deborah shook her head slightly. "I don't know what I'd do without The Saddle Club," she said. "I'll trust you to take care of yourselves, I guess. You know more about horses than I do, anyway—and I want to stay with Max."

"We want you to stay with him, too," Carole assured her.

"Here." Chloe came up with a backpack and loaded it

116

into Stevie's four-wheeler. "It belongs to that guy who stopped to help us. His jacket's inside." She took off her water pack. "This thing is empty now." To Deborah she added, "Please give it to my parents and tell them I'll be there soon."

Deborah nodded. "Mrs. Reg or someone like her will be waiting for the rest of you guys, okay?"

"We're fine," Carole said. "Go."

While they waited for Stevie to come back, Lisa, Carole, and Chloe reassembled the horses' bridles and got them ready to go. Lisa knotted Barq's broken reins together. She stood stroking him. Her feet were still killing her—walking five miles in her boots was going to be agony, but she knew she was in a lot less pain than the horse. *I'll just say my multiplication tables as many times as it takes,* she thought.

Lisa felt a tap on her shoulder. It was Chloe. "Here," she said, handing Whitey's reins to Lisa. "You ride, I'll walk."

"Oh, that's okay—"

"You're limping already. I'm not." Chloe smiled. "I don't mind walking at all."

"We'll switch back later," Lisa promised. She climbed into Chloe's saddle and settled her feet into the strange, broad stirrups. Chloe's saddle felt as comfortable as a sofa. Lisa sighed. "Thanks," she said to Chloe.

Carole suggested that they start moving so that Stevie

wouldn't have to walk all the way back. She took Belle's reins and led her along as she walked Starlight up the ridge. Chloe came next, coaxing Barq, and Lisa followed. When they met Stevie, she had both hands full. "Here," she said, holding something out to Carole. "From the man's backpack. He said we could have them." It was a candy bar.

Carole managed half a grin. "I guess I could eat one now."

12

THE NURSE STEPPED out of the hospital room. She smiled at the four girls and Mrs. Reg. "You can go in now," she said. "Don't stay too long."

"Max!" Stevie's resolution to speak calmly and quietly failed the moment she opened her mouth. "Max, are you okay? You look great! What happened? How do you feel?" She bounced once on the edge of Max's hospital bed, but when she saw him wince she slid off. "Sorry! We're so glad to see you!"

Max was sitting up, supported by several pillows. A large white bandage covered his arm from his wrist to high above his elbow. His hair stuck up spikily, and he definitely

119

looked goofy wearing a light-blue hospital gown. Otherwise, he was almost entirely their own Max. "Same old Stevie," he said with a familiar grin.

"She speaks for all of us," Carole said, giving Stevie a small push so that they could all crowd around Max's bed. Deborah sat holding Maxine on a chair at the bedside. She got up and offered the chair to Mrs. Reg. Lisa took Maxine and cuddled her.

Mrs. Reg refused to sit. "Come, dear," she said, taking Deborah by the arm. "I know perfectly well you haven't eaten dinner yet. I'll go with you to the cafeteria while this crowd has their visit."

"We'll keep Maxi," Lisa offered. "We'd like to."

Deborah paused. "Have all of you eaten? I could send food up."

"They've eaten," Mrs. Reg said. "Trust me." One of the ride stewards had taken them all out for pizza, after she had helped them find temporary stalls for their horses. Even Chloe, her parents, Phil, Mr. Baker, and the Pony Tails had come. They'd eaten six large pizzas.

"Don't worry about us," Stevie said. She moved a little closer to Max. Once Stevie's twin brother, Alex, had been very sick with meningitis. Stevie was ashamed that it had taken Alex's illness for her to realize how much she loved him. She'd known how much Max meant to her even be-

120

fore his accident, and she was very relieved to see him looking alive again.

Lisa took Deborah's vacated chair. Chloe and Carole moved to the other side of the bed. They all looked at Max, and for a moment none of them could speak. Carole thought how grateful she was to have him looking so well. *If I say anything, I might cry,* she thought. *And I am way too happy to cry.* She just grinned at her dear teacher.

"Well!" Max said lightly. "Some sponsor I am! Good thing I took you girls along."

"An accident like that could have happened to anyone," Chloe told him. "We were all walking along the ridge—it was just chance that your horse was the one that spooked."

"I don't think it would have helped if you had been riding, either," Carole said. "Once Barq fell over the edge of the trail, it was going to be bad no matter what."

Max smiled. "That's a relief," he said. "I'm glad I didn't do anything too outrageously stupid. For a while I was afraid I'd been showing off, doing circus tricks on Barq's back or something like that." He laughed, so his visitors laughed, too, although Lisa didn't quite understand what was funny.

"Can't you remember what happened?" she asked.

Max shook his head. "The last thing I remember is kissing Deborah good-bye at the second check."

"But we rode for miles after that!" Lisa said. "That's terrible!"

"Why?" Max didn't seem concerned. "Why does it matter? I had a pretty good concussion," he continued, "but the doctors don't think I've done my head any permanent injury. People often don't remember bad accidents. It doesn't matter. I didn't forget anything important."

"Of course it matters!" Stevie said. "It's perfectly unsatisfactory!"

Chloe explained. "None of us saw what spooked Barq. We wanted you to tell us."

Max grinned. "I guess you'll have to ask Barq." His face fell. "How is the old boy?"

"He's got a bad cut on his shoulder on the near side," Carole said. "The vet at the finish line stitched it for us. He's got a lot of other little cuts, and he looks awfully stiff and sore, but other than that he's okay. He walked to the finish. He's a little lame in front; it looks like he bruised his knee."

"If he's like me, he's pretty sore," Max said. "I feel like I fell down a mountain."

None of the girls laughed. Carole shuddered, remembering Max's head hitting the rock.

"Sorry," Lisa said. "I can tell you meant that as a joke,

but to us it just isn't funny. We *saw* you fall down a mountain. I never want to see anything like that again."

Max grimaced. "I'm sorry, too. I guess it's just as well I can't remember."

"Are you really okay?" Carole asked. "Because, to be honest, you looked awful on that hillside. I mean, we were seriously worried. I mean—" Her voice trembled, and she stopped.

Max looked right at Carole. "I'm seriously okay," he said. "I'm stiff and sore, and I've got stitches in my head. I'm going to have to take it easy at home for a few weeks. But I get to go home tomorrow morning, and I'll be back with my wife and daughter and students and horses. The doctors tell me two things saved me." He pointed to a plastic bag on the lower shelf of his nightstand, and Lisa handed it to him. He opened it and took out his battered riding helmet.

"If I hadn't been wearing this, I probably would have left some brains behind on the rock I hit," he said. "Now you know why I always make you wear helmets. If it can happen to me, it can happen to you."

He cleared his throat. "Also, it seems I was bleeding pretty good out there." He tapped his bandaged arm. "This cut is six inches long and two inches deep, and it nicked an artery. The doctors tell me I lost a lot of blood."

Stevie nodded, feeling a bit sick as she remembered the deep-red puddle.

"People can die once they go into shock," Max said. "If you hadn't stopped the bleeding and hadn't gotten help so fast—if you'd waited for rescuers to find you instead of going to get them—I could have died. I really could have died quickly. So I'm incredibly grateful. But I know I was in good hands. The Saddle Club doesn't wait for people to do their rescuing for them." Max looked solemn and proud.

Now Carole couldn't help the tear that slid down the edge of her nose. Lisa suddenly became very interested in baby Maxi's fingers. Chloe snuffled loudly.

"So do we get three wishes?" Stevie asked, breaking the emotional atmosphere.

"Three wishes?" Max asked.

"Sure," said Stevie. "Isn't that the way it always happens in movies? Three wishes for saving your life?" Carole and Lisa burst out laughing. Chloe looked startled but amused.

"I don't think so," Max said. "I think you've got me confused with one of those genies living in bottles. I might see my way clear to grant you all one wish, but that's positively it."

"A trail ride," Carole said promptly.

"With a picnic lunch," Lisa added.

"No," Stevie said. "I've got a better idea. A round of sundaes at TD's—Chloe included. I promised her we'd take her if we ever finished that ride."

Chloe grinned. "I'd forgotten about that. I don't live too far from Willow Creek—my mom goes there to shop sometimes."

"It's a deal," Max said. "The next time you come to town, Chloe, call, and we'll all go drown ourselves in hot fudge."

"That would be wonderful," Lisa said with a sigh. Maxine tugged at her hair, and she gently pulled the baby's hand away. She felt wonderful. She had to admit that even sitting down on a chair, instead of on a moving horse, was a treat. She had her boots off and her tennis shoes on, her stomach full of pizza, a sweet-smelling baby in her lap, and, best of all, Max wide awake and looking nearly normal.

"You wouldn't believe how fantastic all the people who were running the ride were to us, Max," Stevie said. "Right now Belle and Starlight, and all our horses, are resting in nice cozy stalls at the house of one of the stewards—"

"She's the woman who took us out for pizza—" Lisa explained.

"But not Whitey," cut in Chloe. "I mean, he didn't go for pizza, of course, but he's not at the steward's, either. He's in the parking lot."

"In a horse trailer," Lisa added quickly.

"Well, of course. He's waiting for me. With my mom and dad." She smiled softly at Max. "I probably should go. I promised them I wouldn't stay long. I just wanted to be sure you were really okay."

"Yep, I am," Max said.

"Thanks for being my sponsor. The ride counted, you know," Chloe continued. She lifted the edge of her sweatshirt to show off her new belt buckle. "See? We made it under the maximum time allowed, by something like three minutes."

"Good thing you weren't worried about going fast," Max said with a wry smile.

Chloe laughed. "Yeah. Well, we were doing pretty well for the first forty-five miles. Walking Barq out took the longest. I don't care—you know that—but it's nice to have finished, anyway. So, bye." She suddenly looked a little shy.

"Call us about that sundae," Stevie reminded her.

"I will."

Carole stood up and gave Chloe a quick hug. "Thanks so much for all your help," she said.

126

"You're welcome." Chloe flushed, looking pleased. Stevie and Lisa gave her quick hugs, too, and then she left, closing the door softly behind her.

"So you really finished, huh?" Max said. "That's pretty good, considering all the delays."

The Saddle Club smiled at each other. "The best part was that even Prancer passed the last vet check," Lisa said. Her voice swelled with pride as she thought of the magnificent mare. "Mrs. Reg, Mr. Baker, Phil, and the Pony Tails took care of her while I went back to you. I don't know how they got her cooled down so well and so quickly, but they did. She looks fine now, Max. Even Chloe was impressed—she said she was going to have to rethink her opinion of Thoroughbreds. Prancer looks almost as good as Belle and Starlight. And she ran so hard for you."

Lisa couldn't help smiling as she said the last few words. Prancer couldn't have understood that Max was in danger. *She ran so hard because I asked her to*, she thought. *She ran so hard for* me.

"Mr. Baker took the Pony Tails home with him and Phil," Carole continued. "That was after we went for pizza, which was after, of course, we made sure the horses were comfortable. We'll go get the horses next and drive home."

"I know that much," Max said. "Mom's going to go with you, and Deborah and the baby are staying here tonight.

One of the nurses said she'd find Deb a cot to sleep on. With any luck, I'll see you all at Pine Hollow tomorrow afternoon." He leaned his head back against the pillows, and suddenly he looked very tired. "I keep remembering just one thing. It sounds crazy, but it was something about strings. That rude waitress at TD's wouldn't serve them. She asked one if it was a string, but I can't remember what the string said. . . ."

Stevie grinned from ear to ear. "You remember the joke, Max, I just never got to the punch line. The string said, 'No, I'm a frayed knot!' "

"Afraid not," Max mumbled sleepily. "That's awful."

Carole shook her head. "Of all the things to remember!"

The door of the room opened, and Deborah and Mrs. Reg came in, Deborah carrying some food on a cafeteria tray. "I couldn't make her stay downstairs to eat it," Mrs. Reg said, smiling. "Are you almost ready to go, girls?"

"Sure," they said. Lisa nestled Maxi into her baby carrier.

"Thanks again," Deborah said to The Saddle Club.

"One last thing," Max said as they were leaving. "What happened between you and Chloe? Suddenly you guys all seem to be getting along pretty well."

"Why wouldn't we be getting along?" Stevie asked. "You've no idea how helpful she was after your accident.

128

All that stuff she carries with her really came in handy." Stevie paused, thinking. "I guess she didn't make the best first impression on me, but first impressions can be awfully deceiving. Chloe's great."

"She let Lisa ride Whitey," Carole added. "She really cared about whether you and Barq were okay. Plus, she knows a ton about horses. We have a lot in common."

Max grinned. "I'm glad you discovered that. The, um, first part of the ride, it didn't look like you were going to."

Lisa remembered that after the second check, she had started to like Chloe, but Carole and Stevie still hadn't. She remembered how uncomfortable she'd felt. Maybe Max had felt that way the entire ride. She caught his eye and grinned. She didn't remind her friends that "the first part of the ride" was actually the first forty-five miles or so.

"GIRLS! GIRLS, WAKE UP!" Stevie felt a light but insistent hand shaking her shoulder. "Stevie!"

"Um." Stevie opened one eye. "Oh, hi, Mrs. Reg. Are we home?" She had been asleep in the backseat of Max's truck. Lisa, also asleep, was leaning against her shoulder.

"We've got to see to the horses," Mrs. Reg said.

"Right." Stevie yawned and stepped outside. She nudged Lisa awake. In the front seat, Carole stretched and yawned. Stevie looked around. Pine Hollow Stables was a lovely, welcome sight; even the outline of the trees against the dark sky was familiar. Stevie knew she wouldn't get lost on

130

the trails around here. She shook her head. "What time is it?"

"Nearly midnight," Mrs. Reg replied. She opened the back door of the horse trailer, and Stevie helped her let down the ramp. Carole and Lisa opened the side doors to untie the horses' heads.

Stevie shook her head again. "That's amazing. It's still the same day."

"It's been a long one, hasn't it?" Mrs. Reg agreed.

THEY LED THE tired horses into their stalls. Red had anticipated their homecoming and had bedded each stall extra thickly with fresh sawdust. Fresh grain, hay, and water were waiting.

While Prancer dove her head into her bucket of grain, Lisa got a curry and a brush and went over her one more time. She could hardly believe how well Prancer looked. The mare seemed a little thinner across the rib cage—horses could lose a lot of weight even in a single day—but she would quickly regain that. Lisa groomed Prancer from the tips of her ears to the end of her tail and didn't find any cuts or injuries to worry about. She carefully examined Prancer's feet. The shoe that the ride farrier had nailed back on was holding firm. Lisa dropped the foot with a

131

sigh. "You beautiful darling," she said to her favorite horse. "Thank you so much for everything."

Carole rubbed Starlight's nose softly. He had had the easiest time of all their horses—he hadn't gotten lost like Belle, galloped for help like Prancer, or crashed down a mountainside like Barq. Still, Carole thought, laughing gently, he doesn't have to do any of those things to prove how wonderful he is. Starlight had been great, just as he always was, and Carole was very proud of him.

Stevie leaned her head against Belle's shoulder and languidly brushed her back. Stevie wondered what Phil was doing—sleeping, if he had any sense. Good thing Teddy was okay. She patted Belle one last time before shutting the stall door.

The Saddle Club met at Barq's stall, where Mrs. Reg was carefully and tenderly applying a salve to the gelding's injuries. "Is he okay?" Carole asked.

"He'll be as good as new," Mrs. Reg assured her. "I'll take care of him, girls. I got your sleeping bags out of the truck and put them in the office. Go to sleep now. Good night."

When they had picked up the horses for the trip home, Mrs. Reg had realized how late they would be getting in. She'd called their parents and said that the girls could sleep at the barn. Lisa was very grateful for this as she trudged up the stairs to the hayloft, sleeping bag in hand. The sooner she could get to sleep, the better. That little nap in the truck hardly counted.

Carole flicked her sleeping bag open with an expert motion. "This has been the strangest day of my life," she said. She sat down and took off her shoes, wincing as she did so. The blisters on her calves were unreal.

"The best part—the only important part—is that Max is okay," Stevie said. She tried to lie stomach-down, but her sunburned cheeks hurt too much when she pressed them against her pillow. She flopped onto her back. Much better.

"And that Barq and our horses are okay," Carole reminded her.

"And Teddy," Stevie said, remembering. "Poor Phil."

"I hate to say this," Lisa said, "but Phil sort of had it coming. I mean, he wasn't taking the ride seriously at all."

"I know," Stevie said. "But remember what everyone said. Teddy just might not have been a very good horse for endurance riding."

"Right," Carole said sleepily. "If Phil had learned more about endurance riding, he might have known that. He could have been extra-careful getting Teddy ready, or he could have borrowed one of Mr. Baker's school horses for the ride."

133

"He's learned his lesson," Lisa said. "I'm sure he wishes he learned it another way."

"Yeah," Stevie agreed. "He's learned that Belle is superior to Teddy in every single way."

Lisa reached above her head, grabbed a handful of loose hay, and whacked Stevie on top of the head with it. "Stop that," she said. "I hope this ride taught us all a little humility. I mean, when terrible accidents can happen even to Max, you know they can happen to anyone, no matter how good the person is with horses."

"I know," Stevie said, grinning abashedly. "And Carole, I've got to tell you, I was so impressed with the way you took care of Max today. You really kept your head, and you remembered what to do far better than I would have."

Carole shuddered. "I felt so *panicked*," she said. "I just knew that panic wasn't going to help Max. I was thinking that you did a great job of getting Barq back onto the trail," she added.

"And then there's Lisa," Stevie said. "That last part of the trail was *hard*. After we'd finished the ride, I couldn't believe you'd gotten help so fast. You really did a great job."

"Not me," Lisa said sleepily. "Prancer." Downstairs, Mrs. Reg clicked off the stable lights. The glow from the stairwell vanished, and the loft went dark. Outside the open window, a crescent moon shone.

"Remember the first show you went to, with Prancer?" Stevie asked.

"Be quiet," Lisa replied. The show had been a disaster. Prancer had kicked a judge and had been disqualified from competing.

"I'm only bringing it up to remind you how far you've come. You and Prancer both."

"And then there's Chloe," Carole said with a laugh. "I was thinking about her on the way home, before I fell asleep, and I don't think I liked her until after Max was hurt. Before that, all her helpfulness just seemed like showing off. Afterward, whether or not she was showing off didn't matter. We just needed her help."

"Think about all the ways she was helpful," Lisa said, agreeing. "The water, the sunscreen, the bug spray, Prancer's shoe—everything."

"Think about how annoying she was," Stevie countered. "She was always giving us advice. We're not total riding novices. We know a lot about horses."

There was a moment of quiet while each girl thought. "We must have looked like total novices to *her*," Lisa said at last. "Just the way she looked like a total space alien to

135

us. It wasn't her fault. She was trying to be helpful. And I think none of us wanted to admit how little we really knew about endurance riding. Chloe knew a *lot* more than us."

"I disagree," Carole said. "I don't think we didn't want to admit how little we knew. I think we had no idea how little we knew. We thought since we'd trained hard, we had endurance riding all figured out, but we didn't have the first clue how hard that ride was going to be."

"I agree," Stevie said. "When you really think about it, we were almost as bad as Phil. We weren't prepared at all. I've got raw skin on the insides of both knees from riding fifty miles in blue jeans."

"I've got blisters that'll take weeks to heal," Carole added.

Lisa laughed. "I may never wear high boots again. But let's talk about all that tomorrow. I'm tired. We finished our endurance ride, and we've got the belt buckles to prove it."

"Good thing," Stevie mumbled, as they drifted off to sleep, "because I'm never doing that again."

136

ABOUT THE AUTHOR

BONNIE BRYANT is the author of many books for young readers, including novelizations of movie hits such as *Teenage Mutant Ninja Turtles* and *Honey, I Blew Up the Kid*, written under her married name, B. B. Hiller.

Ms. Bryant began writing The Saddle Club in 1986. Although she had done some riding before that, she intensified her studies then and found herself learning right along with her characters Stevie, Carole, and Lisa. She claims that they are all much better riders than she is.

Ms. Bryant was born and raised in New York City. She still lives there, in Greenwich Village, with her two sons.

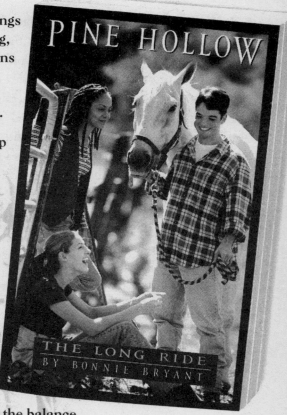